Peter Thomas was born in Hereford in 1954. He attended Hereford Cathedral School between 1965-71. After working in London for three years, he went to Essex University to study English and European Literature (B.A. Hons).

He has taught English in Abergavenny, Greece, and Saudi Arabia. He got his T.E.F.L. in Barcelona in 1990. Since returning from Saudi Arabia, he worked briefly as a carer and, since 2018, he has lived in Hay-on-Wye, the capital of the second-hand book trade, where he still lives to this day.

For Helen.

Peter J. Thomas

THE STAG'S HEAD

AUSTIN MACAULEY PUBLISHERS®

LONDON • CAMBRIDGE • NEW YORK • SHARJAH

A CIP catalogue record for this title is available from the British Library.

ISBN 9781035806935 (Paperback)
ISBN 9781035806942 (ePub e-book)

www.austinmacauley.com

First Published 2024
Austin Macauley Publishers Ltd®
1 Canada Square
Canary Wharf
London
E14 5AA

Preface

Article in local paper.

Local publican commits suicide.

Police have reported the apparent suicide of local publican Ken Reece, seventy-three. Mr Reece, of the Stag's Head in Llawen, shot himself with his old army revolver.

Mr Reece, along with his wife, Beryl, had managed the Stag's Head since the end of the war. He was a popular publican. He and Beryl had been married for over forty years. She died from breast cancer in 1994.

Police had to break into the pub on a tip-off that something was wrong. Milk had not been collected from the doorstep for some time.

The pub is now shut until further notice.

'This is at the beginning of the story.'

'…And so, when a person meets the half that is his very own, whatever his orientation, whether it's to young men or not, then something wonderful happens: the two are struck from their senses by love, by a sense of belonging to one another, and by desire, and they don't want to be separated from one another, not even for a moment.

He whom love touches not walks in darkness.'

This is a quote from Plato.

Chapter 1

Light dawned slowly at the curtain's edge. These January days were increasingly dark and forbidding.

Day after day of grey, sullen skies. It had rained on six of the last eight days; a heavy, forceful rain that had saturated the little patch of grass that Steve called a back garden. No sooner had the grass absorbed one downpour when another stronger downpour came along, rapidly filling up the indentations in the scrubby lawn.

The few snowdrops planted last September in an effort to cheer the place up hung their sad heads as if they were ashamed. The excess water overcame the path leading to the wooden garden shed at the bottom of the garden, and every time Steve went to fetch something from the shed, he had to splash through standing water that bathed his sockless feet.

On such a day, he felt the urge to emigrate to warmer climes in Spain or Italy. He thought back to his army days in Cyprus; the horseplay with his mates on the beach, playing volleyball with the lads, but no sooner had he thought of that, than the sound of the rain on the windows brought him back to reality. The rain dragged him back to England; the rural England; the agricultural rural England which was a stone's throw from the Welsh border.

His alarm clock rang and he stretched to turn it off. It was seven o'clock and he heard the increasing sound of traffic on the busy road outside his home. He went for a run every morning. He might be unemployed and out of the army but he liked to keep up his fitness and his routine. He always kept to the same route; first, along the road to the convenience store then round the side to the children's playing field, then under the railway bridge to the brook, and then back.

It usually took half an hour and then he allowed himself ten minutes in the shower afterwards. After power-showering and towelling himself dry, he looked at himself in the mirror that had steamed up slightly. His eyes were a bit puffy from the night before, the waistline was expanding despite the jogging; even a couple of grey hairs on the side of his short, dark brown hair. He religiously pulled them out.

His beard was well-trimmed and black. He was a handsome cadet who had looked good in a uniform. His legs were still strong, tight, with sturdy calves; the result of running with a heavy pack on his back. So all that training did pay off after all. He thought it might, although he cursed it bitterly at the time. For thirty-six, he still looked good. He could still turn the heads of the younger guys in the pub.

"You're not over the hill yet, mate," he said to himself as he wiped the soap from his face. He found that he was giving himself these encouraging pep talks more and more often these days as if he was beginning to doubt what he was actually saying to himself, but the fact that he was saying it, seemed to calm and reassure him.

He ate breakfast in a tiny kitchen fitted with a grey marble top. On a sunny day, they looked smart, but on a dull day, they emphasised the drabness of the place.

He switched on the small portable TV he had in the kitchen. There was more bad news from Kosovo and more talk about recession so he quickly turned it off. The silence was palpable. He wanted to feel positive about the world today as if it still held something to offer to a young, good-looking ex-soldier with few job prospects.

He had been out of the army for two years now and had drifted from job to job trying to find a purpose in his life. So far it eluded him. Having been dishonourably discharged from the army created problems with employers. That bloody night in Cyprus, what was he thinking of?

Not being able to get a decent reference from the army, he made one up and told interviewers that he had been working abroad in various building sites and campsites, and couldn't really provide references. Not many believed him. He landed a couple of factory jobs but the sheer tedium of them meant that he didn't last long and he was soon back at the job centre signing on.

They got to know him after a while and presumed he was just an unlucky guy who couldn't settle. They'd seen a few like Steve before. It was difficult to see a way out of his predicament that didn't involve going abroad again, perhaps that was the answer. He got a couple of plastic bags out of the cupboard and got ready to go out food shopping.

He heard the dreaded knock on the door again; it was the landlady looking for her rent. He owed her for six weeks.

"Steven, are you there? It's Sharon."

Of course, he was there, where else would he be? He was jobless. He opened the door.

"Hiya, Sharon, how are you?" A buxom forty-four year old blonde met him. She looked angry.

"Don't bother with that," she said. "This is not a social visit. You owe me six weeks' rent, Steven. What happened to the money you promised you'd be putting in for me? I'm disappointed with you. When you came to me looking for a place to live, I thought I'd give you a chance.

"You seemed to be getting on your feet and finally going somewhere, but now you seem to be going backwards. What happened?"

"I am sorry, Sharon. That job just got on my nerves. I tried to stick to it as long as I could but packing boxes is not for me. I'm more of an action man. My life is about action and danger. I'm happiest when I'm outdoors in the wild, not stuck in a factory."

"Well, like this you'll end up out of doors for good because I can't afford to keep you here for nothing. I have to pay the mortgage on this place, otherwise they'll repossess. It's important that you try to catch up with the arrears. Can you at least pay me ninety pounds to go towards it?"

"I'll try, honestly. Let me talk to my mate, Graham, he'll be ringing me this morning. I'll try to get a sub from him. I don't want to go to the loan sharks again. That causes trouble, as you know."

"No, don't go there. We have only just fixed the lock from the last time. Try Graham and see what he says. Is Graham working now? He was looking for an office job last time I heard."

"Yes, he got a job with the housing association. He's a bit bored with it but he's sticking to it."

"Well, we've all got to do things we don't necessarily enjoy, Steve. It's called life. Get a job and settle to it and pay me my rent."

"I will. Very soon now. Don't worry, you'll get your money."

"Ok, do your best, please. I really don't want to chuck you out. I like you; you are a lovely bloke but you need to get yourself sorted out quickly." Sharon wasn't much older than he was, yet he always ended up feeling like a naughty schoolboy when she came around. It was humiliating being lectured to by someone who could have been your sister.

How did a woman a few years older than him come to own three houses anyway? Did she work harder than him when she was younger or was she just lucky?

Did she make a good marriage or win the lottery? He had to admit he didn't know that much about her. He only had dealings with her when he owed her some money. That was no basis for a relationship. He wanted a relationship of equals, but what he got was humiliation on the doorstep. He had to talk to Graham.

He waited until Sharon's car had disappeared from the drive and then he called his old army buddy.

"Graham, I need help."

"Morning, buddy, what's the problem?"

"I've just had Sharon around here again looking for rent. I owe her for six weeks."

"Oops, how have you managed that? I thought you were getting on top of your debt problem. I know it's been tough since you left the army. You've got to find a job, mate. I've told you before."

"Yes, I know, but I can't seem to stick at anything for long. How do you manage that office job of yours? Don't you get bored with it sometimes?"

"Don't I just. About four o'clock in the afternoon, I'm clock-watching till five-fifteen. It's hell really but we all need to bring the money in somehow. With a physique like yours, can't you find a rich sugar-daddy somewhere? I know older men are not who you go for but at least they've usually got a few bob!"

"You make me sound like a tart. I'm not quite at the stage of tossing some old bloke off in the toilets for twenty quid, not quite anyway. Can you lend me ninety quid till my next benefit comes in? You'll get it back, you know you will. It would really help me out, I'm desperate."

"I could in a few days' time when I get paid, but at the moment, I'm down to my last twenty quid. Meet me at the coach, we'll have a few sandwiches and a pint together, and discuss it there."

"Okay, twelve o'clock. Aren't you working?"

"Yes, but I can take an early lunch. It sounds like you need cheering up. Don't be late, I've only got an hour. I'll pay."

"Ok, mate, see you then." Steve felt better already. Graham seemed to have the knack of sorting problems out, finding solutions to difficulties that seemed intractable, he didn't mind lending money if he had to. That was useful. Steve normally paid all the money back, but he knew he did owe him about a hundred already.

Graham had joined the army at the same time as Steve. They did their training together and it was unfortunate that about the same time as Steve was dishonourably discharged. Graham had to leave for medical reasons; the strain of carrying anti-tank missiles affected his back. He was on bed rest and resented leaving the army. He had loved it but it was either that or ending up in a wheelchair by the time he was thirty. The decision was made for him.

After tidying up the bedroom and washing up the breakfast dishes, Steve got ready to go out. He had to sign on that day, buy some food and then meet Graham for lunch. It was some kind of social life. Grey was the predominant colour of his life at that time. Steve's father, who had been a policeman for most of his adult life, always lived life in terms of black and white. He wouldn't understand grey.

If there was a problem, it had to be fixed and there must be a solution for it. When Steve had trouble understanding maths at school, his father was determined to teach him himself. How could he not understand? It was so simple But to an eleven year old, it was baffling, and the homework usually ended up in tears and embarrassment.

It was the same years later when his father tried to teach Steve how to drive. His father was a good driver, and had been driving for the police for years, but he was not a good teacher. Steve had memories of gripping the steering wheel so hard that it hurt as his father barked out meaningless instructions while the car jumped and zigzagged down the country road.

They had to give up eventually and years later, Steve was taught by a professional driving instructress. She was a good female driver and he managed to pass the first time. His pride in that was immense. He felt as if he had really achieved something and driving was a pleasure to him after that. He even drove for the army.

Seeing life in terms of black and white can have its advantages too. You know any problem can be solved but it also has its limitation. Steve worshipped his father and wouldn't have a bad word said against him but he knew that he wasn't like him and couldn't measure up to his achievements. This realisation made him feel inadequate.

He remembered the time when he came last in a swimming competition and his father was in the crowd watching him. He felt his father's disappointment bitterly even though his father praised him and said he had done his best. Maybe this was the reason why he wanted to join the army. He wanted to prove something to his father, that he was just as big a man as he was.

But it turned out to be a mistake. He wasn't really suited to it. He passed the training because he had always kept himself fit but he wasn't really a team player.

He thought he was but there were moments when all he wanted to do was to go off somewhere on his own and think about things. He felt happier then. The lack of privacy galled him and he actually resented the other lads he was with. Their idiosyncrasies annoyed him and their lack of intelligence and curiosity about the world exasperated him. He began to drink more, even during time off, and eventually, overstepped the line on a night out in Cyprus.

That night out in Cyprus. He could still smell the frangipani trees and hear that incessant noise of the cicadas. He was on edge. He wanted something to happen and on that night it happened. After a few drinks, in the NAAFI he headed into town and the bars along the beach.

He went to meet Graham at the coach and horses. It was a backstreet brick built pub with a union jack flying over the door. Steve arrived a bit early. So he ordered a pint from Ray, the owner of the pub and ex-soldier himself.

"Has Graham been in yet, Ray?" He asked as he got his pint.

"No, haven't seen his ugly mug in here yet. Come to think of it, it's a bit early for you, isn't it? Don't usually see you in here till lunch time. What's the matter? Boyfriend kicked you out of bed?"

"Yeah right, you've got it."

"Don't mind me, I am just kidding you. You do what you want, kid. You're young, good-looking. Why should you care?"

"I don't, Raymondo. I'm a free agent. Why? Has anyone said anything about me?"

"Only the usual."

"Why do you let those queers in here, Ray?"

"You should ban 'em. That kind of thing. I don't mind you and your mate coming in here; it's good for custom. Just be careful who you talk to. There are some funny customers in here. Talking about funny customers, here's your mate. Pint, Graham?"

"Hello, Ray, you old tart. How are the other coffin dodgers feeling this morning?" He indicated a group of elderly punters at the other end of the bar.

"Leave 'em alone. You'll be old one day too," said Ray.

Three angry men took their pints to a far table. The pub was clean but basic. There was only one bar so you had to whisper if you wanted to keep anything private.

Gossip got around in his pub. The clientele were mostly men and definitely elderly. They liked Ray because he talked to everyone and made everyone feel welcome, but he didn't allow any nonsense to break out. Any sign of trouble and he sorted it out. Even though he was in his retirement, he could still handle himself and he could rely on a few of the punters to help him out if things took a nasty turn.

Graham and Steve had only ever seen one fight in here and that was between a boy and his girlfriend. She had his hair in her hand and was pulling it hard. She had just found out that her boyfriend had been sleeping with her best friend and that had shocked her. It took some time to get her out of the pub.

She wouldn't let go of the bloke. Eventually, both of them were bundled out into the street still locked in a vice-like grip. Once out of the door, they were forgotten about and a noisy calm reigned in their place.

Such incidents were rare. Drunkenness was common though.

These ex-squaddies could drink a bit. It was mostly beer but Ray did a good trade in whiskies and prided himself on knowing and appreciating a fine malt. The pictures of local soldiers behind the bar, wearing their uniform with pride, set the tone of the place. The boys almost imagined themselves still in the army, surrounded as they were by cap badges and other insignia.

One wall had a collection of Zulu shields and spears there were colourful feathers sadly dangling over the dart board. Pictures from the Boer and the First World War hung over the fireplace.

Ray himself had fought the Mau Mau in Kenya in the fifties and there was a picture of him with a dead antelope and one in his uniform, beaming proudly. Try as they might though, they couldn't get too much out of him about what happened then. He just said that it was a long time ago and the past should remain in the past.

Ray was a tall man and still had the military bearing. He stood erect with his shoulders back; he was clean-shaven and kept his hair trimmed short. He looked magnificent as a young soldier. Steve, although he took the mickey out of him, admired and respected him. He reminded him so much of his father. One of Ray's more annoying habits was to address the pub as if it was a public meeting.

Privacy was impossible to have; everyone knew each other's most intimate business. So when Ray asked Steve if his boyfriend had kicked him out of bed, it was said to the whole pub. However, it was impossible to be offended because Ray was the same with everyone, so it hardly mattered. But if you wanted to keep your privacy intact the Coach and Horses was not the pub for you. Ray had lost a few punters over the years because of it but that "matey, we are all ex-soldiers worked."

Worked for Steve and Graham and they had been coming here for years. The two lads took their drinks and settled at the table near the window. They sat side by side and had a good view of the whole bar from there.

"Do you reckon Ray thinks we're a couple?" Graham asked rhetorically. "He knows you're gay because I told him but does he know I'm straight?"

"Well, you told him that earlier when you mentioned that you had a girlfriend or do you want to keep him guessing?"

"No, not really. He has seen me with Angie in here before so he probably knows I'm straight."

"Or you bat for both sides?"

"Surely not," said Graham.

"Well, that does happen these days; the combination are endless."

"Angie was shocked when I told her George Michael was gay. She was so disappointed. I feel pity for the poor person now. And no, we're not going to have some kind of threesome, so don't think about it. I know what you like."

"Shame. Oh, look who's out here today; it's Brian. Now this boy does sail my boat. Look at the arse on him."

"Stop it, pervert. He is a well-built that I'll give you, that hiya Brian."

Brian was a young student who had befriended the two lads one night. Ray had been to his regimental dinner and the ale was flowing freely that night. Brian wanted to go into education and he wanted every day to be a school teacher.

"Join us," said Steve. "But do us a favour and don't talk about Stalin. My mind is still reeling from all the nasty things he did to the Bolsheviks or was it the Mensheviks."

"Both," said Brian. "Stalin wasn't funny with who he tortured. Talking about torture, what are you two doing in here at lunchtime?"

"Money," said Steve. "I need to borrow some money for my landlady. She is threatening to chuck me if I don't give her ninety. I don't suppose you've got any to spare?" He said weakly to Brian.

"I'll pretend I didn't hear that," said Brian. "I've just seen a lovely copy of Bullock's *Hitler, A Study in Tyranny*. It's only 8.95 in paperback but I can't afford it. I was tempted to pinch it but there were too many people around. I may go back later."

"Don't knick it," said Graham. "That's no way for a prospect teacher to behave. I'll buy it for you later. Why do you have to knick it though? Didn't your grant come through?"

"It has but after I paid for my accommodation, this term's fee and non-debt repayment, I'm back to square one."

"It's worse than in the army it seems to me," said Graham.

"It's not easy at the moment for anyone but it's not going to do your future career good if you got a criminal record in it," said Steve.

"True," said Brian. "I need to find a little part-time job somewhere else. I do a few hours in the student union bar but I need something else. Any idea?"

"Escort work, mate, with your body you could pick and choose your clientele," said Steve.

"Yes, and I got a good idea of the kind of clientele you have in mind." Laughed Brian, winking at Steve.

"I'd be your first student," said Steve.

"Fuck off," was the brief reply.

"Pity," said Steve, warming to the idea. "I'd give you a ride to remember." He winked at Graham. He was only half-joking.

"I bet you would. I'd have a sore arse for a week."

"Gentlemen, gentlemen, why do we always end up getting smutty?"

"Because we're not getting any, that's why," said Brian.

"Speak for yourself," said Graham. "I'm getting plenty though. That is one thing Angie doesn't deprive me of."

"Why are soldiers always so randy?" Brian asked, knowing the answer already.

"You know why. It's the training which makes a bloke fit and you multiply the sex hormones. Look at footballers these days, can't get enough of it. Women are the same. Ever seen inside a women loo? What's written on the locks of the doors?

"Leaves men standing," said Steve. "But getting back to my immediate problem. Where can I find a ninety quid in a hurry? Otherwise I'm on the street."

"Could try working for a living," said Brian helpfully.

"Tried that, it doesn't really work though normally, but I'm getting on a bit now. Come on, Brian, you're a student. You people are supposed to be intelligent; give me some ideas."

"Students are the last people to ask about making money but I will say that these days, you can't go wrong with a job like Ray's. Nothing admirable but must be making fair money even in this backstreet pub. Ever thought of running a pub? The breweries are always looking for people to man their pubs.

"You have to sell the liquor of course but you can make a good sum at it. In fact, in today's paper, there was an advert looking for a manager or bartender for the Stag's Head in Llawen."

"Where is Llawen?"

"About ten miles this side of the Welsh borders. It's a very pretty black and white village and it has a large pub and they need someone to man it. I've got the advert here."

He pulled a local newspaper from his bag which he had over his shoulder and showed it to the two men. They both read it carefully. It said, *Due to unforeseen events, a manager or managers are required at the Stag's Head, Llawen. Terms are negotiable. Riny.*

"Sounds like they need someone in a hurry. I wonder why?" Graham said. "Hey, Ray, do you know why they need someone at the Stag's Head in Llawen?"

"Yes, the guy shot himself about a month ago, I went to the funeral. Tragic. He was ex-army; fought in the war. Ken Reece was his name. He lost his wife to breast cancer about a year ago and it really affected him. I met him at a victualler do here in town just after Beryl died and he looked awful. He was trying to put a brave face on but you could tell it was an act. Beryl meant the world to him.

"She waited for him to come back after the war and then they stayed there for forty years. It was a good pub too; quiet and clean. They made a good team for a few years. Ken kept a good pint and Bengal pies, and pastries were legendary, especially on date nights. When she died, he tried to carry on for a bit but the place got dirty and things got out of hand; it became a bit of a heavy boozers place.

"The police had to be called once or twice to set things out after hours. They threatened to take his licence away from him if things didn't improve. I think he had a fire breakout there one night and had to call the fire brigade.

"Next thing I heard was that he had shot himself using his old service pistol to do that job. He never got around to handing it in after the war. There were a lot of people at his funeral. He was a popular man; Ken was great for sure."

There was silence in the place as Ray recollected what had happened. The Second World War was beginning to look like it was a long time ago and the bravery of the men and women involved were like the acts of superhuman to hear about. Ken and Beryl's story seemed cruel and unnatural, and it turned the listener into thinking.

"Well," said Graham. "It's dead man's shoes, do you want to fill them?" He looked at Steve.

"Sure but I still need to make some money. Could we man the pub together, you and me, the two desperados from A company, privates Steve Watts ang Graham Smith." Steve said and Graham smiled.

"There are three of us," said Brian. "I might be interested as well and I probably know more about naming a beer than either of you two together. I serve in Student Union Bar don't forget."

"So you do," said Steve and the way he said it, suddenly the prospect became a realistic one. Steve was already working out practicalities.

"They probably need an experienced manager or something. Maybe they need a deposit," said Steve, desperately trying to pour cold water on the idea.

"It doesn't say so in the advert," said Graham. "It would not cost anything to find out anyway, would it?"

"I suppose not. Let's give it a go."

Suddenly, it didn't seem like a crazy idea. Other people had done it. They were three intelligent men who liked pubs and company and were willing to learn. How difficult could it be? They decided to ring that day.

Graham needed to go back to work, and Brian had other commitments, so it fell on Steve to make the call. He tried to sound cool on the phone as if he wasn't actually that interested.

"I'm ringing about the advert in the paper for a manager wanted to man a pub. Can you tell me a bit about the job?"

"Sure." It was a young man on the other end. "It's an old place in a village setting. The pub is called the Stag's Head and due to unforeseen circumstances, it needs a manager or managers as quickly as possible. Are you ringing for yourself or a friend?"

"Both. There might be three of us interested in running the place."

"Oh, I see. Do you have experience of running a pub?"

"Not really, but one of us works in a student union bar, would that count?"

"Well, any experience of the pub trade is useful. Can you tell me why you're interested in this position?"

"It sounds like a bit of a challenge and I'm ex-army, so I relish a challenge. It could be a change of path. We all are looking for direction." There was silence on the other end.

"I see. Well, let me have your contact details and I'll put more information in the post for you. You will be working for a brewery called Southern Ales and the application will go to them initially."

"That's fine."

"One thing I should say is that the place is a bit run down at the moment. Obviously, the brewery will help with the refurbishment but there might be quite a lot of clean-up jobs needed to be done. Are any of you keen on DIY?"

"Painting and decorating are no problem."

"I also should tell you that there was a small fire in one of the bedrooms upstairs and the damage hasn't been rectified yet."

"Oh, I see. Well, we'll have a look at it and see how much has to be done. You say it was a small fire so it doesn't matter. We'll take it from there."

"Sure. Try to fill them in as quickly as possible!"

Steve put the phone down. Fire damage. He hadn't been expecting that one but possibly the brewery would handle that one. He rang Graham to report the proceedings.

"Fire damage? How bad?" Graham asked.

"He said a small amount of damage. Maybe Ken had it in his bed or something."

"Well, until we've seen it for ourselves, we won't know. Tell me when you receive the application forms and I'll come read and fill them in with you. Do you think we are doing the right thing here?"

"Are you having second thoughts about it?" Steve asked.

"No, but it may be too much for us."

"Come on now, can it be too much after some of the situations we faced in Cyprus?"

"Yes, but we got trained for that and we were younger then; don't underestimate the age factor. There was no fear in those days."

"True but let's at least have a look at the place. If the damage is excessive, we'll walk away from it and pretend it never happened. Assess the situation on the ground and act accordingly, that's what the army taught us, do you remember?"

"Yes, black and white, no grey; as your father used to say. Maybe he was right. Every problem has a solution so long as you look have had enough of it. I think we're going into business together."

"I do hope so. Suddenly, my life seems as if it's going somewhere again. I'll ring you later."

Steve hung up and tried to imagine a country pub with fire damage and all sorts of unlikely reasons presenting themselves to him. He imagined a total wreck with burned-out tables and chairs still smouldering. He imagined the air smelling of cinders and ash. He predicted blackened walls and smashed windows from a fire caused by an electrical fault.

Or maybe just a bit of water damage where the fire brigade had to put out a chimney fire. That wouldn't be too hard. He just didn't know what to expect.

One thing he knew to expect though was the daily bills and demands for money from his creditors. Each day, a new batch of reminders about payments arrived. Some of these demands were accompanied with threats in case of non-payment. Ever since he had left the army, money had been a problem.

He hadn't been particularly well paid in the army but he had kept his head above water. Now he seemed to be drowning in debt and there seemed to be no way out; no way except working to free himself. He was a child of his time though. Most people seemed to be in some dire situation that he was in like it was a case of feathers flocking together. Was he happiest in the company of people who had not much money between them?

In which case, these people couldn't really be of much use to him.

Brian was broke but he was a student. Graham had money but not much. This scheme to own a pub might be the answer to a lot of problems. He just didn't want to mess it up!

That night, Steve couldn't sleep so he got up and looked out of the window. There was a sharp frost outside and the full moon lit up the estate in a ghostly image. A lone dog barked somewhere as he looked down the road.

One or two stragglers from the club were making their way home. He watched a young had been sick in a hedge. The night left him anxiously affected. He would be seeing a lot more of that sort of thing in the future. He was looking at it purely as a business venture.

If people wanted to make themselves ill on his ale, he was not responsible, that was their look-out. He felt no sympathy for them. It was three o'clock before he went back to bed. It had been a long day. That night, he dreamed that he was playing with a fruit machine and he lined up three Jacks. It paid out a huge jackpot. It was an omen.

Chapter 2

The next day, the doubt was still there. Were they doing the right thing? Were they about to make a fool of themselves? Whenever Steve had a serious decision to make, he headed for one place, the river. The river flowed through the centre of the town and a lazy bend provided the ideal place to walk from the ancient bridge and descended gradually to the river bank past a popular pub, The Green Man.

He was tempted to go in and try a pint. It wasn't his usual pub but he was thirsty. The pub was an old one. It attracted visitors to the town because of its age and position by the river. Steve wanted to keep a clear head so he resisted having a pint. There were two young and attractive women drinking outside and they threw him a glance but he ignored them. He had some thinking to do.

As he walked towards the fast moving river, he noticed the general surrounding of the place. The litter had been discarded carelessly, a half-eaten sandwich was being pecked at by a seagull, and old bottles and cigarette ends lay around the benches. The benches had been thoughtfully placed by the council to enable people to come and admire the view. The litter spoiled that somewhat.

The next thing to catch his eye was the bishop's palace on the bank, opposite a large Jacobean building. It was quite beautiful with its own lawn leading down to the river. A lone gardener was cutting the grass with a ride-on mower and Steve sat for ten minutes watching him. The drone of the machine and the regular toing and froing as he and the grass lulled Steve into a drowsy state.

It was mechanically repetitive work that would probably have annoyed Steve after a while if he had been doing it, but he enjoyed watching the gardener, not wishing to be close to them. All bushes and trees were left with a wild fringe around them, which was useful for insects and birds. The house itself had fine large windows that must have provided fine settings for functions and receptions given by the barhops.

"Come out onto the lawn," the bishop would have said to his guests. "Admire the river."

A little flight of steps led down to the water's edge from the garden where probably, in days gone by, a boat would have been tied to provide the bishops with a safer means of transport, especially during the Civil War periods. The town had been royalist but parliamentary forces took it over for a while.

The elegant chimneys on the roof were distinctive of the Jacobean style. They were curled around the top and finished off with a frieze of strange creatures. The house must consist of a number of rooms with large fireplaces judging by the number of chimneys, Steve tried to imagine himself living in these, not the bishop and his family.

He tried to imagine his work. What exactly did a bishop do? They presumably ran the daily life of the church. His place of work would have been the impressive cathedral at the front of the property, his home was a Jacobean palace.

He must feel happy with his life surrounded by so much beauty. Or after a while did he not notice it? Do we get used to beautiful objects and eventually fail to appreciate them? Did the Greeks ever get tired of looking at their wonderful temples and amphitheatres?

This negative thought brought Steve back to reality and he decided to move on. All along the river bank, he heard the drone of the mower, and then suddenly, it stopped.

The river itself was quite high and fast-moving. There had been a lot of rain recently and it had brought down branches and other debris from further upstream; some of which got caught in the willow tree branches that stood at the edge.

One or two swans in and out of the trees after feeding on the vegetation but it wasn't easy for them because the river was flowing fast. So he just watched them, elegantly swimming against the tide, arching their elegant necks and occasionally dipping them below the water to look for fish. These birds added something to the view and seemed perfectly at peace amongst the overlapping willows and the undergrowth.

Steve liked the idea of these birds making a mate for life and he envied them. Where was he going to find his mate?

He cornered the old pedestrian bridge that led to the castle Green. He climbed a flight of steps shaded by trees and came out of the Green itself, which was a large place of open ground surrounded by beech trees. It was the old motte and bailey of the original castle since destroyed in the Civil War.

It was not easy to make out the old castle walls that were surrounding the Green, as nothing of the original stone walls remained. Perhaps if you dug around the vegetation, you could come across some stones still remaining but they lay dormant waiting to be revealed.

The rest had all been grassed over. A group of noisy boys were kicking a ball about, calling each other and laughing. He sat down to watch them. Suddenly, he had a vision of his own school days. He and his friends had played exactly as these young lads but it was twenty years ago. The time gap was suddenly real.

A lot had happened to him since his school days! The army, the foreign travels, the fighting. Where were those friends now? What had they gone on to do? He had a sudden urge to meet them again. Andy and Chris and Phil were his friends.

"Kick it back, mate," one of the boys shouted. Steve realised they were talking to him. He seemed to have dozed off and the ball had come in his direction. He got off the bench and gave the ball a good kick.

"Do you want to play?" One boy asked.

"No, you're all right, lad, but thanks anyway," he answered.

He went back to his own thoughts. What should they do about the pub? On one hand, it seemed like a no-brainer; after all, what did they have to lose? On the other hand, they could lose everything. What if no one comes to the pub?

The public could be very fickle, but not as long as they served good food and drinks in the pub. Steve had finally made up his mind. There was no turning back. He went back the same way he had come. Council workers were busy picking up the litter and cleaning the benches.

Every problem had a solution. The same two girls were chatting outside the pub but this time, he talked to them.

"Would you two ladies like a drink something again?" He offered and they accepted.

"Someone's in a good mood," said one of the girls.

"Yes," said Steve. "I've just solved a problem." He grinned at them and left them to drink.

"Graham, we're going for it," he said on the phone.

"I thought we had already decided that," said Graham.

"We had but I just wanted to be sure, and now I am."

"What persuaded you?"

"Some boys playing football."

"Right ok," he said doubtfully but he knew better not question it.

Steve's moods and thought processes worked differently from other people's. They weren't always logical but he had learned over many years not to analyse too deeply. He just accepted it.

"So, what is the next step?"

"Go and see the place and decide if we like it. You'll have to drive us. We'd take Brian if he is still interested. Have a look at the place from the outside."

"I'm free tomorrow. I've got a day-off."

"Perfect. Pick me up early." The die was being cast and the Rubicon was being crossed. There was still time to back out if they didn't like the look of the place. It all depended on the trip out to seal it.

They could get the keys from the agent just after having a look from the outside. There was a lot they could learn just from that. How bad the pub had been allowed to deteriorate? How much work was involved in getting it up to standard? At last, Steve felt he had something to get his teeth into. His life seemed to have a purpose again.

Steve would have been a useful companion to Robinson Crusoe. The whole business of improving the island and husbanding it would have greatly appealed to him. He rang Brian.

"Brian, we're going tomorrow to see the pub. Can you come and give us your views?"

"Yes, great, but don't come too early. There's a beer festival in the student union bar tonight, So it could be a late one. I have got a good feeling about this plan of yours though. This is one of your better ideas. I think this one will work. If I decide to join in with you, I expect to be an equal third partner if that makes sense with as much say as you two! I just don't want to be treated as an afterthought."

"Brian, we wouldn't do that. You've got more idea about the job than we have. We are going to be coming to you every five minutes asking what we should do. Of course, you're a key member of the team. You're the only one amongst us that knows how to change a barrel. Your knowledge will be invaluable."

Steve put the receiver down and started to feel positive about the whole venture. It all depended now on the state of the pub.

The following day, it rained again. An annoying drizzling rain that got down the back of your neck. Graham turned up on time in his Vauxhall Vectra, which he had owned for five years now and was his pride and joy. Steve opened the door. Graham was dressed in jeans and a Liverpool football shirt. He looked up for it.

"Morning, partner. Ready?"

"Morning, but do you know where Brian lives? I'm not sure."

"Yeah, he lives in that gloomy block of flats in Frederick St. I went with him one night after the boozer. It's a bit rough. It's more like a squat. He didn't even have a front door, courtesy of a police raid a couple of months ago. Luckily, Brian didn't have anything on him at the time but they turned the place over."

"Oh shit, he is into drugs? I hope he doesn't do that at the new place. That's all we need. Well, we will have to make it clear to him that I don't want this to be a druggy pub."

"With the way things are going around here lately, we may not have much choice. But anyway, I really don't think he's into anything heavy. We're not talking about crack, cocaine here. It's a bit of dope and maybe the odd Mandy in a Saturday night, that's all."

"Well, he's going to have to put a stop to that, that's all I'm saying."

"We might be just about to see a lot more of this sort of thing in this trade. There aren't that many youngsters who don't indulge these days."

"Punters, yes, but he's management now or wants to be. He'll have to clean his act up. Have you filled the tank up?"

"Yes, I've got plenty of petrol but it's only ten miles down the road. Relax, breathe. We're only going to have a look. We're not signing anything."

"I know. I'm a bit worked up about the whole thing. I do feel a bit nervous about it. I really want it to work. Sad, you know, I've had a few false starts lately but this one feel different somehow."

"Just come with a critical eye and look for faults. Don't be fooled by a bit of climbing rose around the door. This is a business venture. Money involved. But even if it doesn't work, we walk away to lick our wounds and do something else. I've got more to lose than you, don't forget. I'll have to give up my job. If we take this on, I'll have to give a month's notice. I'll be there in the evening but not in the day."

"That shouldn't be a problem. I am sure I and the boy wonder can cope with daytime trade. It's the evening that's the problem. What if we get some bother there? Some of these customers can get violent."

"Well, then we have to use our army training. We're both lads so to speak and we can handle ourselves. What about that fight that developed in the NAAFI at that time in Cyprus? We were watching a football match with 'C company', do you remember? It was me and you that sorted that one out and worked together, kept our heads and minimised the damage."

"Oh, yeah. That was some night. That was the night I went into town and picked up a guy in the harbour bar. He was good-looking, so had to. You know he wanted money for it."

"Of course, he did, he was trade. You really can't spot 'em can you?"

"Maybe but I'm just not used to paying for it. That cost me my job. I don't really want to remember that. Let's go and meet Brian and then see the Stag's Head. This should be interesting."

They drove over to Hardwick building to the block of flats where Brian was living. It had a worn-down look about it. They walked up to the third floor to Brian's and through where the door should have been and into his bedroom. The place was a mess. It smelt of stale cigarettes and Indian pale ale. Brian was under a duvet sleeping quietly.

His clothes were around the bed where he had dropped them, and books and magazines covered the bedside table which had anglepoise lamp on it. An old stereo system lay on the floor and revealed albums out of their sleeves littering the carpet. There were candles everywhere; a couple of them still burning.

They were on the window sill. A couple on the small bookcase and one even on the bed frame at the bottom of the bed. The air smelt of incense that was sickly sweet. A smell that was a reminder of the happy days in the sixties and was undergoing a revival.

The walls were covered with posters announcing bands that were to appear and one of a matador facing a large black bull. There was one framed photograph of a family holiday by the seaside with twelve-year-old Brian in swimming trunks eating ice cream. All seemed close and content. The boys let him sleep a bit longer. They went into the kitchen to make a drink.

"Fucking hell, is this how he's living?" Steve said picking up a plate with a half-eaten meal congealing steadily in it. He tried to find two clean cups but had to settle for two glasses that had to be washed.

"It's a bit of a shit hole, isn't it?" Graham said. "I remember it was rough from the last time I came but I don't remember it being this bad. Why doesn't he empty his rubbish?" He looked disdainfully at the bags of rubbish in the corner of the room.

"Oh my God, look at this." Steve had just opened the fridge door to find a collection of mouldy sandwiches, half of them well past their use-by date and a bottle of an evil smelling milk. The shells of eggs. The fridge had not been cleaned for some time and it was covered with tomato ketchup and yoghurt. Funny enough, there were two twenty pounds in the freezer section.

"That's weird; what are they doing there?" Steve asked.

"Hidden there in case he gets robbed, I guess. There's no security here, so that's the problem."

"Let's get him up. This place is depressing me."

Brian was already awake after he heard the two men in the kitchen. He was reluctant to get up as he felt warm and comfortable but the two lads encouraged him by pulling off the duvet and throwing his clothes at him.

"Brian, how can you live like this?" Steve said.

"Yes, it can get bad but as Quentin Crisp used to say, after the first five years, the dust doesn't seem to get any worse. Pass me my shirt, will you? It's a few days old but it'll do. We're not going anywhere post, are we? We're just going to look at the place, right?"

"Yes, but the agent is going to meet us there, so make an effort, Brian. I'll get a clean shirt from the wardrobe." Steve opened the wardrobe door and a collection of shoes, trainers, vests and pillowcases fell out.

"Do you have a clean shirt, Brian? I can't see to find one in here."

"I'll wear my jogging outfit. That's fairly clean."

He had a quick shower and dressed in the blue tracksuit and blue fleecy top. He pulled on a pair of white trainers but didn't bother about the socks.

"Quick cup of coffee and I'm ready," he said while Steve had been examining Brian's book collection as he waited. It was an impressive collection of history, poetry and drama. He selected a book by W. B. Yeats.

"I didn't realise you read a lot of poetry," said Steve.

"There's a lot of things you don't know about me," said Brian. He took the book out of Steve's hand and turned the well-leafed book to the poem, *Who goes with Fergus?* He recited the first verse.

> *Who will go drive with Fergus now,*
> *And pierce the deep wood's woven shade,*
> *And dance upon the level shore?*
> *Young man, lift up your russet brow,*
> *And lift your tender eyelids, maid,*
> *And brood on hopes and fear no more.*

"Who was Fergus?" Steve asked.

"An ancient Irish king who gave up his throne to study poetry and philosophy. You can borrow my books if you want when we're working together."

"And you can borrow my soap and hair shampoo, you scruffy git. And get your hair cut." Steve laughed but he was only half-joking.

"Is this how it's going to be?" Brian said. "You two bullying me together?"

"Not at all," said Graham. "We're only kidding with you but you could smarten your act up, young man."

"I'll try," said Brian. "I really will. I want this project to succeed as much as you two. Just give me a bit of space. I'm younger than you and perhaps will be a bit more in touch with a younger crowd. You need me as much as I need you."

Graham and Steve were thoughtful at this moment. They realised Brian had a point and they both began to take him a bit more seriously.

They all got into Graham's car and set off. The rain had begun to ease a little and as they took the Hay Road, they all began to relax.

"The agent said he would meet us there about one. We could have a quick look around before he gets there."

"Good," said Graham. "I want to check out the garden and the brook beyond the garden. If we do take this place, we're getting a lot for our money. The pub has got four bedrooms and also a function room. It used to be an old stagecoach inn and the stables are still there. There is a garden and also a brook that eventually goes into the Wye."

"Sounds interesting," said Steve. Turn right about half a mile on the sign pointed for Lewes.

They were motoring through a very picturesque part of the Wye Valley. The fields were bright green after all the rain that had fallen. They went past many green fields with grazing cattle and sheep.

The cattle all looked well-fed and healthy. The beautiful brown and white of the Herefordshire breed was the only colour on a grey drizzly day. The sky was full of leoden grey clouds hovering above them. The light was dim. The hedgerows were broad but carried the remnants of last year's birds nest.

At one point, they passed a neat church surrounded by a stone wall. Two yew trees stood at the entrance way and the gravestones were at odd angles in the churchyard. An old woman bearing flowers watched them as they drove past. They saw few other signs of life.

The rain kept most people indoors. Only those with jobs to do braved the January weather. The cottages they saw were mostly the traditional black and white and would have been labours' cottages in a time gone by, but many of them now were holiday homes bought by people outside of the county and lived in maybe for half a year. The rest of the time they were empty, locked up and left after the holiday.

They had been done and looked wonderful but there was no life in them. The garden was pretty though.

Brian was listening to them talking and was oblivious to the surroundings.

"Should be round the next bend?" He shouted and he tapped his fingers on the driver next in front of him.

Llawen appeared just as he predicted. It was a pretty black and white village containing one main street and a war memorial at the junction where the road forked; one was the road into Hay and the other would bring you to the village of Clyro.

The Stag's Head was nowhere to be seen.

"Where's the pub? Have we missed it?" Graham cried.

"No, take the Hay Road to the right. It's about half a mile further."

That was the first surprise of the day. The pub was not in the village.

That could be a good thing as it would have no neighbours to deal with. It was going to be a proper country pub.

About half a mile further, the pub appeared. A large 'To Let' sign had been placed on a nearby wall and the place seemed bigger than either Graham or Steve had imagined. It was a traditional black and white Welsh-style long house and over the years, further grounds had been added on to make a substantial property. The sign saying it was the Stag's Head was displayed over the front door.

The entrance to the car park at the back came before the pub and Graham drove straight into a large tarmacked space behind the pub. He parked the car close to the back door and all three lads got out and stretched their legs. They wanted to take their time with this and try to look appropriately at this as it was a potential business venture. All romantic notions had to be disregarded.

The first thing Graham noticed was the state of the paintwork. The wall had been white originally but was now a dirty grey colour. The window panes were all in poor condition.

A couple of panes remained and they all needed to be painted. The lads went to the back door and peered through the glass. It was the kitchen. It was big with plenty of cupboard space and a large prep area.

"The kitchen seems to be ok," said Steve, trying to see past the reflection of the grey and hills behind.

"Hard to tell," said Graham. "It may need a complete refit."

"You used to be able to get a decent meal here when Beryl was alive?" Brian said. "I came here once for a Sunday dinner with my family. It was a good meal."

"Well, that's a good sign at least," said Steve. "To cook a decent Sunday dinner takes time and space. You need good ovens."

"You need to be a good cook too," said Graham, trying the door handle. It was locked.

"Let's take a look at the front."

The front of the property was impressive. The pub sign of a leaping stag with a full set of antlers was painted over the front door. The door itself was studded and painted black with a large door knob in the middle. It looked rustic and comforting as if to say to the people living here that they would be safe in its hands.

There were no curtains in the windows but it was difficult to see much detail inside; although, Graham said he could see a large fireplace. There was a square chimney at the end of the property with four pots on it.

"Haven't seen anything to put me off yet," said Graham. "I wonder where the fire was."

"My money's on the kitchen," said Steve. "Most fires start in the kitchen area. I remember that from the fire safety class I did at my factory job. We shall have to do regular fire drills too."

"Of course," said Graham. "What time is it? Where's the agent got to?"

"It's a quarter to one. We could go and have a look at the garden."

"No, let's wait until he arrives." They sat down at one of the three tables and chairs placed along the front of the pub. They were all spattered with bird droppings and hadn't been cleaned for some time. They were all struck by the silence of the place.

A couple of rooks were flying along the road and the sound of a tractor could just be made out, but apart from that, it was quiet and peaceful.

"We're in the sticks all night," said Graham. "It seems a bit too quiet for me. There is not much passing traffic."

"It's perfect," said Steve. "We'll liven it up a bit."

"We're going to have to make food to make this place pay," said Brian.

"True, but we wanted to do that anyway, didn't we?" Steve said.

"Yes, most pubs offer food these days," said Graham. "If necessary, I'll get Angie involved. She loves cooking and knows a lot about it!"

"Do you think she'd be interested?" Steve wondered.

"Well, we won't know until we ask her."

The sound of approaching tyres turned their heads down the road and a green 4x4 door opened up. A young man in a grey suit got out.

"Hello, how long have you been waiting long? I'm Julian." He shakes all their hands. "Did you have trouble finding the place?" He asked.

"Not really," said Graham. "Although, we were surprised that it isn't in the village."

"Yes, that surprises everyone who comes out to see the place. We have had quite a few people come out in fact but some think of it as a challenge. We had a couple turn up last week who wanted to rent the place but thought being isolated might be a problem. The wife didn't drive and they had two small children so there might have been a problem with shopping.

"There is a small shop and post office in the village but it's a good way to walk there and back, so they turned it down. Pity because I think they could have made a go of it. She could have learned how to drive to take the kids to school, but never mind, onwards and upwards. Have you lot managed a pub before?" Julian asked quizzically.

"No, but we all are keen, aren't we, lads?" Graham said.

"Yes, we all want to see this work," said Steve. Brian said nothing.

"Well, let me show you around," said Julian.

He led the way to the front door and unlocked it. All three men were slightly nervous at that point. It was like they were buying their own property; the expectation was high. Julian stood back to allow the guys to enter. It was a bit like going to church. You entered the gloom from the light.

The guys found themselves talking in whispers. It was quite dark inside. They were met by a long bar running almost the length of the room. A door led to the kitchen at the back and on one wall was a large open fireplace that still contained the ashes of the last fire. Old settles clung to two of the walls and the rest of the furniture consisted of both tables and chairs with beer mats still lying on them.

The smell of stale beer and cider was palpable. Cobwebs had formed on the window and the surface was dusty. On the long oak bar, knots of wood vied with dark stains to decorate the top. The beer taps seemed modern. Shelves still were full of bottled beer and juices lined in the back and a couple of pictures of Ken and Beryl pulling pints hung disconsolately. The edges of the photo were beginning to curl.

They might have been thirty years old. A rather old grandfather clock lay silent next to the fireplace. The room would not have been changed in its appearance much in the last forty or fifty years. A heavy quiet reigned and it probably felt very similar when Ken took over the place just after the war. He obviously was traditional and didn't like to alter much.

Julian put some lights on. A weak light from a naked post bulb struggled to illuminate anything.

"It's better without the lights on," said Steve and Julian switched them off.

"First impression?" Julian asked hopefully, looking at the boys in turn.

"It's perfect," said Steve. "It's actually just as I imagined it would be. It's actually a bit bigger than I thought it would be."

"Really?" Julian said.

"Where is the fire damage?" Graham asked. "I don't see any here."

"It's upstairs. Ken, towards the end, was in the habit of drying his cloths and tea towels in his bedroom over an electric fire. One night he must have forgotten about them and he left them. They caught fire and destroyed the room. We can see that later; come and see the kitchen first."

Julian wanted to show them the best bit and they went through a pair of swing doors to reveal a modern, fully-fitted kitchen. There were eight cooking burners and three ovens. Beryl had obviously taken this side of the business very seriously and had installed many cookers and ovens to provide well-cooked food that the pub could enjoy on a large scale.

She seemed to have been the brains in the partnership. A large fridge-freezer and cupboard took up a lot of space but the central island was perfect for food preparation. It was the best thing they had seen no far.

"Impressive," said Graham, opening cupboards to reveal ample storage space. "What happened to the cat?" He indicated to an empty cat bowl on the floor by the back door. There was a cat flop too.

"Not sure. He could have wandered off when Ken died. Perhaps he is in the stables at the back."

"Chances are he hasn't gone too far," said Brian, a confirmed cat lover. "I bet he will reappear when we take the place over."

"If we take it over," Graham corrected him.

"What's not to like?" Brian said. "Coming from a young guy, be positive. It's got everything we're looking for."

"Let's see the fire damage first," said Steve, not wishing to get carried away.

"It does go downhill a bit from here," said Julian as he led the way upstairs. The back stairs were just off the kitchen and they were quite steep. They led to a long corridor that ran the full length of the building with four bedrooms and a bathroom leading off it. All of them overlooked the back of the property. They looked at the fire damaged room first. The carpet was completely destroyed.

Unfortunately, the fire had spread to the curtain and a dresser nearby. The curtains were destroyed and what was left of the flowery pattern hung limply from the rail. The dresser though was just ruined on the side and could even be repaired. The smoke had blackened the ceiling and the walls, and there was still a faint acrid smell in the room.

"Is that it?" Graham said looking for signs of more damage.

"Just the carpet and the curtain? He must have discovered the fire quickly."

"Yes, luckily there was a fire extinguisher nearby so the damage was limited. The brewery will of course help with repairs and replacements. We are insured for this kind of thing. We don't expect you to cover the cost of that. We will redecorate and put in new carpet and curtains. This old dresser will probably be thrown out."

"Not necessary," said Graham. "A good solid piece of work and I can repair that."

"Really?" Julian said in his annoying manner again. "I'd have thrown it out myself but if you think you can do something with it, I'll make a note to the owners."

"The beds seem to be a decent size," said Steve. "Are they all a doubles?"

"One is smaller. Perhaps you could turn one into a private sitting room or study," said Julian. "Although, there is a sitting room downstairs behind the bar."

"Oh, you didn't show us that room."

"No, it's locked, unfortunately. The police still have the key. They haven't finished their investigation yet. That was the room they found Ken's body in. He shot himself in there."

"Yes, we heard about that."

"Oh, you did? Who told you?"

"The landlord of our local pub knew Ken apparently and even went to the funeral. He said Ken was a smashing guy, ex-soldier and all that. He suggested that things went downhill when Beryl died," said Steve.

"Yes, I believe that's right. He lost the will to carry on. He should have retired, although it would have been a lonely retirement. Beryl meant the world to him. Obviously, if you do decide to take the place on, and I hope you do, you'll get the key back when the police have finished with it."

When that was over, they moved towards the bathroom. It was dated and a strange colour so that would have to be replaced, but the bath was a good one with a shower above. Next to the bathroom, at the end of the corridor, was a window that overlooked the far end of the pub. They could see a building partly absorbed by trees about forty metres away.

"What's that?" Graham said. "Is it part of the pub?"

"Sort of," said Julian. "It's the old stable. This was an old coaching inn remember? They had to have somewhere to keep the horses. There's room for about four-five horses there. Do you want to see it?"

"Yes," said Steve. "It might be useful. We could always rent the stable end. There must be quite a demand for stabling in this area you would have thought."

"Absolutely. Although, check first with the brewery to see if they have any objections. They may have to change the insurance on the place if you're thinking of doing that. It's a good idea though. I see you are trying to work out a way of making a bit more money from the place. There's nothing wrong with that."

It didn't take long to view the stable. A row of ash trees hid the stable from direct view and access was through a small gate in the fence. The stable hadn't been used for some time. The pub probably hadn't been a coaching inn for over a century now. The age of the combustion engine and the steam train had seen to that but people still rode horses and paid good money to do so.

As they came out of the stable, Brian noticed another path leading away from the stable and pub towards the fields at the back.

"That goes to the garden and the brook. It's quite a big brook and it empties into the Wye eventually. There are trout in it I believe."

Julian led the way along a narrow path which went through a small arch of apple and plum trees. The leaves were off the trees and hadn't been swept up for a season. A part of the orchard had been used as a garden. A couple of empty chicken coups were stacked up against a wall.

Somebody, probably Ken, had grown potatoes and carrots judging by the remains of a few plants scattered haphazardly. These plants were busy rotting away in the winter rain and the whole garden looked rotten and neglected. Beyond the garden, they could hear the rustle of fast-flowing water. A large muddy brook meandered its way through the bottom of the garden, eventually emptying itself into the Wye a couple of miles away.

A couple of deep pools looked as if they might be useful for fishing. The recent heavy rain had muddied the pools and it was difficult to see anything in the brook but it looked deep in parts.

"Are we allowed to fish in it?" Graham asked.

"I don't see why not," said Julian. "It's on the pub's land so it's probably ok. I will check with the water bailiff who knows fishing rights as they can be a legal minefield. You can probably catch a few trout at least. Well, that's about it. There is not much else to see, although I forgot to show you the cellars.

"There was no light in there last time I tried to go down. It's a very standard cellar. I'll show you where it is." He led the way back to the pub and showed them the cellar's door entrance in the ground not far from the kitchen door. Steps led them underground and Graham went down to have a look.

It didn't take him long.

"That's fine. There's plenty of room. There are a few barrels in there now. Do you know what they are?"

"No idea," said Julian looking at his watch. "I'm afraid I have to go now. I'll lock the pub up and let you alone for a last look round. Ring me when you make a decision about it. I really think you could make it between you. Your army training plus Brian's expertise should mean you've got everything covered.

"The brewery does lay on short courses for prospective tenants so you can ask a few questions and hopefully avoid a few pitfalls. Many people order too much beer in the first few months and can't shift it. The brewery will help you to get it right. I hope to hear from you soon."

He shook all their hands and drove away, leaving the lads in silence again. The rooks resumed their cawing in the roof.

"Well, fellas, what do you think?" Steve asked.

"I like it," said Brian. "It has got everything laid on. Ok, it needs a bit of work to bring it up to standard, but I think it's on. Count me in any way. Might have to ask Angie to come in for the food side."

"Yes," said Graham. "Although, when she is in the kitchen, she'll love it. There's nothing a girl loves more than free rein in a well-stocked kitchen. She can experiment with the menu too. What do you think, Steve?"

"Oh, you know what I think. I'll move in tomorrow if possible. We're going to do this then? Do we have enough money to do it? I'm broke, don't forget."

"We know that. That's pretty much why we're considering this venture, to get you out of a hole."

"Sounds like the brewery will pick up the tab for repairs though," said Graham. "That will save us a bit. Shall we drink to it? I've got a couple of bottles of ciders in the car." Graham went to retrieve two full flagons of cider and clinking the bottles, the three lads cheered the success of the Stag's Head under new management. The rooks cawed in agreement.

Chapter 3

The next stage involved Angie. It was clear early on to the boys that none of them could cope with the demands of the kitchen. None of them had any skill in that department. And while Steve could make a decent Sunday lunch, it wasn't going to be enough to run a busy pub trade. That's where Angie came in. She was Graham's girlfriend.

They had been going out together seriously for three years now; although, they had met each other in school. When Graham got discharged from the army, he took a number of local jobs and at one of these, he met Angie. She was a department manager at that time and initially gave Graham a hard time, but eventually, she came to recognise him for the hard grafter he was, she began to praise him in front of the other workers.

Angie wasn't above a bit of flirting and Graham realised quickly that he had found an ally and eventually, a friend. They started going out together and they enjoyed each other's company. So much so that she moved into his flat about a year after dating him. She made it clear to him what a huge compliment she was paying him by trusting him like that and he repaid her by being faithful to her.

It didn't come to his mind to look for anyone else. It was lucky that she liked Steve because Steve and Graham did come as a package. It was a bit like living with both of them because Steve was often on Graham's mind and he asked Angie her opinion concerning his mate on a number of issues.

She pretty soon stopped trying to set Steve up with dates from work and accepted that he wasn't the marrying kind. She thought it was a huge waste seeing how handsome he was but some fish just slip through the net. Anyway, she had caught her fish and was busy reeling him in towards the keep net. Graham tackled her about the pub.

"We've been to see the pub I was talking about," said Graham.

"Really?" She sounded receptive and turned the page of the magazine she was reading.

"Yes, it's not bad. It needs a bit of doing up now but it has a large kitchen space and a dining area."

"That's nice. I always wanted a decent-sized kitchen," she said dreamily, not really understanding the direction the conversation was going in.

"Yes, Steve and Brian agreed too," he persevered.

"Yeah, that's good."

"So much so that they were genuinely interested in taking it on." He eyed her keenly.

"What? You lot run a pub." She put her magazine down and faced Graham head-on. "Are you kidding? I can't see Steve sticking that for long though."

"No, it's in a beautiful location. It's got four bedrooms as well as a stable block. Weren't you always saying you would like to own your own horse someday? Well, now's your chance. You could have three or four."

"You want me to move in with you to the pub?" She said with a rising level of alarm in her voice. "What about this place?"

"Not just move in, work on some side of things. If we have a weakness, it's not having enough knowledge about cooking. We need someone who can run the beautiful kitchen and prepare good pub grub. We all thought you could do it."

"Yes, but what about my job with Cooper's? I've just been promoted to manager with good pay. I'd have to be foolish to give all that up and I couldn't manage two jobs. I'd be knackered for both of them. No, I don't think it would work. Not that I'm totally against the idea, it might be fun to run a kitchen with you three, but I don't see I could do it."

"Not even if we employed a kitchen porter to help you?"

"Well, that could help. Brian could probably fill that role. Half the problems are of preparation rather than the actual cooking. I could help out in the evening if you were busy but a full-time commitment, no, I don't think so."

"Well, don't dismiss the idea just yet. Sleep on it and tell me in the morning what your decision would be. We really want you to be part of the team."

"That's your army talk again. Your blessed team work. I am a team player, though at least I always thought I was. I will think about it and decide later. You could always open the pub without offering food for a while," she said helpfully.

"True, true," nursed Graham. "But we would have to offer food at some point. Most pubs do these things and it seems to make a difference between success and failure." They let it lie there for a while.

Steve meanwhile was busy filling in the application form. When it came to declaring previous jobs and the reason for leaving them, he came to a halt. Should he mention that he had been dishonourably discharged from the army after a night of passion on the beach with a boy? Probably not! It didn't look good no matter how you dressed it up.

That night had been a mistake. Maybe if he had paid the guy, it would have been all right. The guy wouldn't have complained as he would have got his money and everything would have been fine. He remembered much about the sex part. They were in a lonely cove in dark, hidden from view by rocks that were edged the beach.

The boy had a good body and Steve genuinely wanted him. They had kissed passionately for a while. Steve, emboldened by Dutch courage and the kid's willingness, had stripped the boy off. He could remember being enraptured by the size of him and the boy moaned in genuine pleasure as he lay under Steve.

However, when it came to paying the lad, things took an ugly turn. The boy wanted more than he had originally asked for and Steve didn't want to be taken advantage of. They argued, Steve hit him once on the chin and the boy reported him.

The next day, Steve was up in front of his commanding officer. He didn't deny that he had sex with the boy; it seemed childish to do so. He could tell that the officer was angry. He talked about letting down the regiment and letting his company down. Steve couldn't look him in the eye. About a week later, Steve was out of the army for good.

So better keep this from the application form. The rest of the form was pretty much straightforward. He made it clear that there were three of them interested in running the pub but that his name would be on the licence. He rang Graham when he had finished.

"I've just finished filling in the application form. I didn't mention anything about the army incident. They're not likely to find out, are they?"

"I wouldn't have thought so. Who have you put down as a reference?"

"Sharon said she would be one. I think she'll be glad to see the back of me. I have caused her a bit of trouble. The other one is my old English teacher, Mr Donald. Do you remember him? I rang him up and said that he would be eligible to be a referee. He doesn't think I'll make a go of it but was willing to do it. He wished me luck with it."

"Oh, I remember Diddley. Didn't he like to run his hands through the boy's hair in class? He'd end up in court for that these days."

"Oh, well, at least he proved himself to be of some use. Well, we have to provide him with a few free pints when we're open. Yes, he knows the pub. He's visited it a few times. He might become a regular."

"Watch out then, he's got you pinned. He'll have his hands down your front in no time."

"If he's lucky he will. Anyway, I'm off to post it now. Anything you want to add?"

"Only to say that Angie might be coming in part-time. She really doesn't want to give up her job. We may have to run the pub without offering food for a while. It's normal but there is a chance she may change her mind later if we make a go of it."

"Typical but she has got a good job already. I can understand why she might be a bit reluctant. It is a big step to take after all." Steve put the phone down and left to post the form.

As he dropped it in the letterbox, he said, "Good luck." He heard back within a week. It turned out that there was only one application for the job. No one else thought that the pub was going to run. At a time when pubs were folding at an alarming rate when money was in short supply and people's drinking habits were changing, to take on a place like the Stag's Head could be seen as a risky venture.

But businesses didn't always have to be logical and make sense. There was always room for commitment, innovation, and dare he say it, romance. That could bring something quick and new to the equation. That's what Steve said to the area manager at the interview. Mike Powell managed pubs in the Hereford and Worcester area for southern breweries.

Steve and Graham showed up for the interview at the head office On Ledum Rd. It had itself been a brewery twenty years before and the walls of the office were covered in old black and white photographs of a brick building holding large vats and containers. The men were smartly dressed in white aprons covering their new working clothes and there seemed to be an orderliness about the place.

They knew what they were doing. They had been brewers for years and that experience bred a confidence that the beer would always end up being drinkable.

It must have been difficult in those days to regulate temperature and recreate the same conditions necessary to brew a good pint. But the tradition of brewing went back centuries in this country. Most houses brewed their own beer and because the mash had to be boiled, the drinking water was cleaner and healthier because of it.

Young boys would be sent to the pub with large pitchers to provide beer for thirsty working men. Agriculture labour would have a flagon of cider to wash down their ploughings. Alcohol was in the national DNA.

Mike was keen to know what the three were planning for the pub. Who was going to do what? He had spent his whole working life around pubs. He would be the man they could deal with if there were any problems. He could predict the problems before they happened.

"Don't worry if the business doesn't take off immediately. This pub hasn't made any money for over three years now. Ken lost the plot when Beryl died and there were some problems with the police on a number of occasions. They had to be called when things got out of hand usually when Ken let a few of his cronies stay after hours.

"It's important to stick with the correct opening and closing time. If you try to change these too much, people will take advantage. People like to feel secure in a pub and to think that the bar staff know what they're doing. You two haven't had much experience in that regard."

"True," said Graham. "But our army training means that we're organised and ready to combat any problems that arise. The army teaches you to problem solve and I'd say we're both good at that. Wouldn't you agree, Steve?"

Steve had been looking at the window, worried about saying the wrong thing but he agreed with Graham.

"Yes, Mike, the army taught us a lot of useful skills and I'm sure they'll come in handy while running the pub."

"Skills such as?" Mike inquired.

"Such as how to handle aggressive people," said Steve. "We both have done defence courses and can handle ourselves if you know what I mean."

"It could be useful," said Mike. "But if there is real trouble, we prefer our staff to contact the police. It's their job to sort out aggressive customers and you will meet some people like that. Don't serve anymore if you think they've had enough. Be strict about that. It's better to lose a disgruntled customer than risk a situation developing into a brawl.

"Most fights occur between people who know one another. Get to know your customers and their concerns, and that will be half the battle. Many people go to a pub just to meet other people and socialize, especially in a village setting. Obviously, a lot of your customers will come from the agricultural community.

"Their concern is the state of the roads and the wages of labourers. Try to get interested in their way of life and don't say too much yourself. It's funny what can annoy people. A lot of them won't actually be too interested in anything else. It's a chat and a laugh and a joke that interests them. For some of them, this is their only social life.

"Don't get too friendly with them. It will take time to get to know them of course, if they like the way you're running the place, they'll come back and turn into regulars. Are you interested in serving food?"

"Eventually," said Graham. "But now straight away neither of us is a good cook. Although, my girlfriend, Angie, has offered to lend a hand. She already has a job at Cooper's in town, but if the pub is successful, she might come in with us.

"Both me and Steve will be serving behind the bar and also a student friend of ours, Brian. He is the only one with experience because he serves in the student union bar at college."

"That would be useful. Does he know how to change a barrel?" Mike asked.

"Yes, he's done that many times."

"Doesn't matter because we teach you that on the week-long induction course. We teach all our new tenants. We'll teach you the basis of hygiene, keeping the pipes clean, organising the till and ordering stock. You'll soon get the hang of it. Have you got any other questions for me at this stage?"

"No, I think we've covered most things. Are you going to give us a chance?" Graham asked.

"Oh, yes. The position is yours if you want it."

Steve gave out an involuntary yelp and held out his hand to Mike.

"Thank you, Mike. You have no idea what this means to us. It's like a fresh start for both of us."

"Well, good luck, lads. We'll be in touch with a proper contract for you to sign and then you are officially the new landlords of the Stag's Head at Llawen. Congratulations and good luck."

They all shook hands and had a small drink to celebrate.

There had been no awkward questions, no embarrassing silence or shifting in the chair. The interview had been a success. Both men were surprised at how easy it was. The technical side of things wasn't going to be a problem. At most, it was just hard graft. Steve looked up the Stag's Head on the internet.

A lot of information was on it including some history of the place and the small part it played in the Civil War. Being a coaching inn, it had access to a blacksmith with a forge. One story said about the forces of Prince Rupert rested near the pub one night in 1646, and had used the blacksmith and forge to shoe horses and repair tack. Repairs to armaments were also carried out there.

The inn was subsequently renamed the Royal Stag's Head for services to the king's force. It lost the title during Cromwell's time. There was also the story of a ghost being in residence in the 18th century. It seems that a young man from Llawen was hanged for stealing sheep and was made on example of to stop thefts in the neighbourhood.

The ghost of the young lad was said to haunt the bar at night, especially at harvest moon time in September. The pub was acquired by Southern Breweries in the 1930s and had been tied to the company ever since.

The landlady Beryl, at times, was said to offer a range of pub grub and Sunday lunches. Children and pets were welcomed and there was a picture in the front of the pub with directions on how to get there. A full-length picture of Ken and Beryl smiling proudly was at the bottom of the page with the logo of 'the best beer in the marches' underneath. There was no mention of what had happened subsequently.

It was obviously some time since the page had been updated but Steve thought it was good to put it in on the net. He wondered if it had been Beryl's idea. Their next job should be producing a new page announcing the change of landlord. Steve wasn't sure what to make of the ghost story but many old pubs had similar stories linked to them.

Pubs used to be courthouses and were also used as execution sites often and had a noose hanging over the stairs. Thus, seemed to be where most of the ghostly incidents were seen. Anyway, it should add more character to the place. Steve only hoped that Brian wouldn't be too freaked out by it.

He closed the page and called Graham.

"Seems like we have a ghost. A young lad was hanged in the pub in the 18th century for stealing sheep."

"Interesting. Well, it adds a bit more colour to the place. Any news from the brewery yet?"

"Not yet but it shouldn't be long now."

"I just want to move in now. I can't wait to hand my notice in from this place. I've had enough of other people's housing problems. Is there anything we should buy do you think?"

"Like what?"

"Well, a new washing machine might be useful. Didn't see one in the pub when we were there."

"No, now you mention it, I didn't see one either. We'll need a good one too with all those tea towels and clothes to wash. We don't want to be smelling of beer all the time. Perhaps we should look for a good one now."

"Meet me in town later."

Later that afternoon, they bought a new washing machine and the move began to seem real to them. They were going to be publicans and run their own pub after all. They began to get excited at the prospect. The place where they bought the washing machine was an out-of-town shopping precinct full of large warehouse-type buildings that catered for just about every consumer's wish you could think of.

There were hi-fis by the hundreds, cameras to set up a whole photography industry and racing bikes to equip a thousand eager cycling groups. Not much was displayed in the windows; it was mostly posters there but inside was an Aladdin's cave of bright new goods.

That say that the Celts loved bright shiny objects and there they were in front of them. Everything was laid out in big shining rows. A whole aisle of washing machines stretched out ahead of them. It was hard to choose which one would be best but was a test of the close relationship between Graham and Steve that they rarely argued.

They were like a couple who had survived the first seven years of living together without coming to blows and who have settled down to the large house along with bringing up children, buying the house, regularly changing the car and perfecting the rose bushes in their small garden.

It helped that they had been friends at school and shared a common past, and of course, had been in the army together which was something of a dangerous situation. They felt comfortable in each other's company and while walking down the long aisle of gleaming machines, they offered each other advice and made recommendations.

"We need to get a big drum as much as we can afford, maybe 7Kg," offered Steve.

"Agreed. This black one is nice. It's a washer-drier, could be useful," said Graham looking inside the drum.

"I prefer Hotpoint, it has got more settings," said Steve.

Families with children in tow wandered there. The parents occasionally arguing, berating their children for touching the goods.

"Don't touch that, Michael," said one exasperated mother to her five year old boy who was turning one of the dials. "You might break it." She pulled him roughly away and the boy began to cry.

Steve had done this trip with an old girlfriend of his but that relationship was turning sour and there was the beginning of bitterness on both sides. However, neither of them was brave enough to finish it, so they walked sulking between the rows, one regretting the presence of the other. They had been talking about setting up a flat together, and though they should start with a washing machine, it was soon obvious that they would never agree on anything.

They didn't seem to have anything in common. They walked apart and at one point, ended up in different aisles. They failed to find a machine that satisfied both of them and left the shop feeling angry and disappointed with each other.

The frustration was easy to see on both their faces and the relationship broke down soon after. Steve and Graham meanwhile came to a decision on the Zanussi which seemed to do everything they needed it to do and was not too expensive. The company would deliver it to Graham's place later.

Having got the business part settled, they walked off to get cheeseburgers and a drink at a fast-food outlet nearby. Steve found a seat near the window and watched a busy Saturday unfold outside. Graham went off to order two meals. The place was crowded and many children were crying and arguments were breaking out between the parents. Everyone seemed miserable.

Buggies blocked the aisles and Steve surveyed the whole scene and sighed. This was the day when most people had time-off work, time to enjoy themselves with their families and they inflicted this on themselves. He waited patiently for

Graham to bring the meals but because of the queue, it took some time.

Steve watched the weary crowd scurrying around with trays of food and drink. Graham didn't need to ask his mate what he wanted; he already knew. Steve always ordered the same thing—a large cheeseburger with side salad, fries and a medium coke. Graham usually choose the chicken and had a fruit juice.

If either had ordered something different, the other would have asked if there was something wrong. They might as well have been married to one another.

An argument began between a man and his young daughter at a nearby table. The girl seemed to be upset about something and was crying bitterly. Her father became angry with her.

"Just wait till I get you home," he shouted. The mother looked embarrassed but didn't interfere. Steve couldn't help himself; he had to say something.

"Hey, mate, calm down. You can see she's upset."

The man looked over angrily.

"What's it got to do with you? She's got ketchup all over her new dress. I warned her about that." As if to prove his point, the man showed a small amount of ketchup on the girl's lap.

"Ok, but she's just a kid. Don't be so hard on her. All kids make a mess of something or other. I'm sure she didn't mean to." Steve smiled at the girl who had stopped crying, grateful to have an ally on her ride. She stole a shy glance at Steve.

"Keep your nose out, mate. Have you got kids of your own?"

"No, but what's that got to do with anything?"

"Well, when you've had your own kids, then you can tell me how to bring up mine. Meanwhile, back off." His tone was getting angrier, so Steve left it at that. He just hoped that the girl's mother would stick up for her own daughter tonight when they got home. It made Steve shudder. There was still a tense atmosphere when Graham eventually appeared with the food.

"What's up?" He asked shooting a glance at the nearby table.

"Nothing, just an arsehole taking it out on his kids."

The other man pretended not to hear. He didn't want to take on two men so gathering up his family, he ushered out of the restaurant.

"Can't leave you alone for two minutes without starting an argument," said Graham.

"I hate guys like that. It's so easy to bully young kids. I wish blokes wouldn't do it. It's like some men are angry about being married perhaps because they feel trapped. Why do they get married in the first place?"

"Well, you don't know the full story. Perhaps his bank manager is on to him or he owes the taxman something. You never know what goes on behind closed doors."

"I'm not sure I want to," said Steve. "It reminds me of my father bullying me about my maths homework. The state I used to get in over that. Anyway, how much did this lot come to? I'll go halves with you when I get my benefit money."

"Forgot it. We'll settle up when we're both earning!"

"Cheers, Graham. You are my best mate you know that, don't you? I wouldn't consider going into business with anyone else apart from you. You know that, don't you?"

"I do now. Eat your meal, yer daft twat, before I lay one on you."

Both men stopped talking and ate in silence for a while.

"Do you think you'll ever get married?" Graham asked between mouthfuls.

"Doubt it," said Steve. "I like lads too much you know that." He looked around to check that no one was listening.

"Well, just don't like them too young if you know what I mean," said Graham looking at some of the boys nearby.

"Don't worry, that doesn't turn me on, thank God. Actually, it disgusts me. I like them when they're old enough to vote and drink."

"Yeah, but that's getting younger all the time. Just stay the right side of the law that's all I'm asking of you. Don't embarrass me. You're my best mate, I want you to be the best man at my wedding whenever that is. I don't want you to do anything foolish that's all I'm saying.

"We've been through a lot together and I want this business venture to succeed for both our sakes. Promise me you won't decide to pack it all in after three months." He looked seriously at Steve.

"Hey, relax. I'm in this for the long haul. You can depend on me. You can trust me with your life, remember?"

"I remember, and I'm glad of it. But you haven't managed to stick to anything for long since the army. Why is that?"

"Good question. I think it's because leaving the army the way I did knocked my confidence. I'm still not over it like it's unfinished business as far as I'm concerned. You know how much the army meant to me, to us both.

"It provided a security that was missing at the moment. You got up when they told you to get up, you ate when it was time to eat. I liked that you didn't have to think too much."

"I know what you mean, but we're on our own now so it's up to us if we succeed or fail," said Graham, giving a steady look at his friend.

"Failure is not an option, believe me," said Steve.

They finished their meals and gathered up the trash left behind. It all got emptied into a huge bin already half-full of partly eaten chicken and burgers. It suddenly seemed a terrible way to spend one's time.

"When we get our pub up and going, we'll offer a much better eating experience than this," said Steve, looking around in disgust.

"Let's hope so," said Graham, swinging the doors open and breathing out into the fresh air.

Chapter 4

The letter informing them that they were successful in getting the pub arrived two days later. They were expected to attend the week-long induction course at the brewery and Brian volunteered to attend alongside them. Needless to say, Brian outshone them in everything apart from the ordering of the stock and the financial side of the business.

Graham did the best at this. Steve was good at ideas to upgrade and encourage new business. Some of his ideas were very innovative. He even suggested an armed forces' night where members of the services could claim free drinks if they could prove they had served abroad.

Your average soldier, sailor and airman had a thirst which could be good for business. The brewery seemed happy with this idea and all three completed the induction.

The first job now was to clean the pub from top to bottom.

They turned up at the pub that first weekend armed with brushes, brooms, cloths, dusters, and detergents. They had the desire to clean the place in preparation for their opening night. Angie had come along to give a hand. It needed that woman's touch to really clean the place properly; to fit curtains and blinds; to get the drains sparkling and the wood shining.

It hadn't been cleaned for some time. They decided to start in the attic and then work their way down. The attic was accessed via a step ladder through an opening in the ceiling at the end of the corridor. Graham and Steve volunteered for this job. They took up a dozen black plastic bags expecting to find a lot of abandoned stuff and boxes of clothes and items stored there over the years.

They weren't wrong about that. There was no light in the attic so they worked with a torch.

Both men gingerly looked through the dozens of boxes and bags left in a heap by the previous tenants. Most contained clothes, some dating back to the forties and fifties. There were a number of old suits. As Ken aged and his body changed, his suits were abandoned as he couldn't fit into them. All of them had the distinctive wide lapel fashion famous at the time.

There were a number of women's blouses, frilly and patterned, which would have been a nightmare to iron. There were a number of brown wigs. Beryls hair had fallen out due to the cancer treatment and she had been anxious to hide the result. These got thrown through the opening to Brian underneath, who bagged them up. He was fascinated by the style of the clothes.

Opening bag after bag was like going through time travel of the fashionable history of Britain since the war. Wide lapels gave way to no lapels and jeans gave way to shorter and shorter skirts. After a while, the style stayed the same. Ken and Beryl gave up on fashion and just settled for comfort.

"Wow, did women actually wear this kind of stuff then? We could throw a great forties night and get dressed up in all of this. Maybe we shouldn't throw it away yet," he said eyeing fox fur complete with head and paws.

"This is gruesome through." He put it around his shoulder, the paws dangling pathetically on his chest. He paraded up and down the corridor in it, pulling the fur closer to his face. It had a rather musty smell which put him off.

"I wonder if they will ever come back into fashion?" He said finally throwing it into a bag.

"Hope not," said Angie. "Surely our days of wearing dead animal has gone. Foxes, pheasants and rabbits are much nicer when they're running around." Nobody disagreed with her.

Next to come down were old boxes of beer mats and about thirty pint glasses. Tea towels and a couple of old dart boards next made an appearance. All the materials required for running a country pub were stored up there. Crib boards, dominos and shove half penny boards saw the light of day, as well as footballs and a lot of shirts and shorts.

Ken must have loved his football and encouraged the locals to play other pub teams. All of it looked as though it dated back to the fifties; the old leather balls and the long shorts. There was something sad about it all ending up stored here.

Then, Graham made a discovery.

"Well, I'm blown away. So they kept it after all."

"What's that?" Brian shouted through the hole.

"Hang on, it's quite big. Give me a hand, Steve."

A lot of pushing and pulling could be heard, accompanied by some swearing from Steve as he caught his finger on a nail.

"Fuck, I'll need a plaster for that. This is heavy. Do you think it'll go through the hole?"

"Well, it came up here so presumably it'll go down."

Through the hole came a large wooden pub sign with 'Royal Stag's Head' written on it. A picture of a leaping stag accompanied the lettering.

"That's interesting. This place was called the 'Royal Stag's Head'," said Brian. "I wonder why?"

"It was called that during the Civil War," said Steve. "In recognition of the help given to the royalist force at the time. I looked this place up on the internet and found out quite a few interesting things about it. Did I tell you it's supposed to be haunted?"

"Woah! No, you didn't," said Brian. "You didn't mention anything about a ghost. A ghost of what exactly?"

"Of a young lad from here who was convicted of sheep stealing in the 18th century. If it had been a hundred years later, he probably would have been transported to Australia, but as it was, he was found guilty and hanged downstairs in the bar."

"Now, that is seriously creepy. Why didn't you tell me about that earlier?"

"We kept it quiet because we know what you're like. You would have freaked out and maybe not come with us. Just treat it as an interesting incident. It adds character to the place and gives it a sense of history. It happened a lot in those days."

"An inglenook fireplace adds character to the place. A hanged lad gives it bad luck. How many others were there?"

"Nine as far I know. They were cruel times back then; justice was swift and merciless. We could do with a bit more of that these days if you ask me," said Steve.

"Luckily, we're not asking you. I always thought you were a hanger and a flogger. I bet you'd have been the first one to operate the old ducking stool and throw rotten eggs at some poor sod in the stocks," said Brian. "This sign needs a good clean, perhaps touch-up the paint work, but otherwise, it's in good condition. It's a better one than the one on the door. Could we swap them over do you think?"

"Mmm, not sure they'll let us do that. The Royal Stag's Head does have a better sound to it though," said Graham.

"Let's do some research on that and see if there would be an objection to it," said Steve. "I don't suppose the brewery would mind. Lots of places have royal in their name, why shouldn't ours?"

"Yes, but it's usually for service to the royal family like purveyors of jam or biscuits. This place just shooed a few horses as far as I can make out. I'm not sure that warranted a royal title."

"There's more to the story, I recall," said Steve.

At that point, Angie called up to them to come and have a break.

"Are you scrubbers ready for a break yet?" She yelled from the bottom of the stairs. "I've got your teas and coffees here." They trudged downstairs covered already in cobwebs and dirt. The break was very welcome.

"Found any Da Vinci's up there?" Angie asked quizzically.

"No, but we have made an interesting discovery of the old pub's sign. We might swap them over. What have you been up to?" Steve asked.

"Trying to get this kitchen in shape. I've done the oven and cleaned out the cupboards. Came upon a fine bone-china tea set. Could have been a wedding present maybe. You don't see them around much now. They've gone out of fashion but you can still pick them up in the charity shops though."

"Blame the tea-bag for that people prefer a good-sized mug these days," said Brian, helping himself to another couple of chocolate biscuits.

"Have you finished in the attic?" Angie asked. "I could do with a bit of help here. The surfaces and the floor need to be disinfected."

"Ok, just let us finish the attic. I'll probably hoover up and try to get rid of the dust. There are only a few old books and ornaments left up there. We could leave them there," said Graham. "We are grateful for your help, babe. Perhaps after the kitchen, you could make a start on the bar?"

"Right. Brian can help me with that after I've had a cigarette."

"Smoke it outside please," said Graham. It was one of the few habits of his girlfriend he hated; that and her obsession with chocolate.

"Come on, Brian. Bring your lighter."

She and Brian went outside and sat on a bench in the overgrown back garden looking over the car park. It was her chance to get to know that young student better. "Thank God for a fellow smoker here. I always feel guilty lighting up around Graham. I get the evil eye whenever I go near a packet of cigarettes or a Mars bar."

"Oh, you like chocolate as well. There really is no hope for you. These two are very clean living, aren't they?"

"Yes, maddeningly so. Don't mind me asking but you're not gay too, are you?"

"No, I like girls. Did you ask because of Steve?"

"Yes, I was really surprised when Graham said he was gay. You can never tell these days, can you? The most unlikely men turn out to be gay."

"Yes, it seems to me that the more masculine you are, the more likely you are to be gay. Steve came across to me as a typical army bloke but there are times when he shows his more sensitive side. I'd love to know why he got thrown out of the army. Neither of them will tell me anything. They think I'll blab it around the place," he said archly.

"I do, Graham told me. I can't tell you though without his permission. I sure wouldn't tell anyone."

"Oh, go on, tell me. I'm dying to know," he whined.

"Exactly. You may keep a secret but I'm not so sure. Perhaps when I know you a bit better. It's really is not that bad. I think he had a tough time there. I don't think he deserved to be discharged. It was sexual, I'll say that much." She gazed into the distance and Brian knew he had gotten as much he could out of her. At this, he stopped asking questions and gazed at the garden. His eyes focused on a strip of grass that looked odd.

"What's that mound of grass there? Look." He pointed.

"Oh yeah, could be a rubbish mound or a compost heap that's been covered over."

They both went to investigate. It was a mound surrounded by a ditch that had a few shallow puddles in it.

"It's a duck pond," said Brian. "It's been allowed to dry out but it's a pond all right. I wonder if we could rescue it and fill it up again. I'd love to have ducks splashing about. What do you think?"

"I think you're right. Really this place is full of surprises. It's bigger than you think when you look at it from the front. It goes back a hell of a way and it has some features that were missed the first time you looked at it. I think the lads would love to have a duck pond; the eggs might be useful too. Makes a change from chicken all the time. How could we fill it up?"

"Either from the kitchen or from the brook. The kitchen would probably be easier. It would have to be dug out a bit first through. That's another job we can add to the list."

They announced their discovery to the two lads and they were both delighted. That afternoon, they tackled the bar.

Ken hadn't bothered much with cleaning the place after Beryl died. He seemed to lose heart a bit. Years of beer stains and cigarette marks had to be tackled. Not all the stains could be removed but at least the long bar looked cleaner. Indentations in the wood on the top of the bar were the result of the drinkers sloshing cider as they got their pints.

After the first sip, their hands steadied somewhat. The acid in the drink ate away at the wood and it must have eaten away at them over the years. The décor of the bar was dated. Old photos, some dating from the fifties, were removed but not thrown away. Brian refused to throw away anything of historical interest.

He said he'd keep them in a scrap book. Probably many of the men in the photos were dead by now. At some time in the future, the whole bar would be redecorated, but at this time, it was more important to get the room clean. Tables were wiped and rearranged to get a couple more in.

Mirrors were polished and floors were scrubbed. Angie got a couple of vases from the kitchen and put them in the window.

There were no fruit machines or games machines of any sort in the pub and the boys were happy to keep it that way at least for the time being. Farmers were usually too careful with their money to gamble it away.

After a couple of hours, the room looked and felt much fresher. They replaced all the light bulbs with stronger, brighter ones that had the effect of pinpointing the cobwebs. They all got pleasure from cleaning the old pub, but why? What force was at work in them which drove them to scrub, polish and clean; it was more than that.

By laying a hand on the place, made it somehow theirs. It became their property in a way it wasn't before. This sensation was very real to them and they worked towards cleaning all the two hundred pint glasses they discovered behind the bar. In a number of them, spiders had taken up residence and a good number of dead flies and wasps were visible too.

The glasses which were washed and polished were stocked along the shelves ready for use. It was beginning to resemble a real working pub. By four o'clock, they had all had enough, so they rested with cups of coffee and packets of chocolate biscuits for comfort. Steve in particular was delighted.

"Well, what do you think?" He asked rhetorically as he surveyed the room from the bar.

"It's coming on," said Graham. "It's a lot cleaner than a lot of places I've drunk in."

"It's cleaner than our union bar," said Brian, rolling another cigarette.

"Don't congratulate yourselves too soon, we haven't tackled the toilets yet. Steve saved the best for last," said Angie taking her out from Brian and producing her packet of cigarettes.

"Yes, we have to take great care with the toilets," said Steve.

"If one thing can turn customers away, it's dirty toilets. I'll have a go there."

"Don't forget there's an outside toilet as well around the back," said Graham.

The outside toilets were useful. It was by the car park and it contained a urinal with two cubicles. Steve took a scrubbing brush and bucket of hot soapy water into the dismal scene. The basins were grimy and dusty. They looked as if they hadn't been cleaned for years. He worked away on them and made them gleam.

He went into one of the cubicles and suddenly took a step back. Drawn on the back of the door was all sorts of obscene pictures of naked men. They had greatly exaggerated penises that entered men bending over; huge hairy balls sticking out provocatively.

Steve caught his breath. It wasn't that he hadn't seen such drawings before, it was just that he hadn't expected to see them here.

There were a number of messages to ring these numbers for sex. There was others saying that Jonson or Ben or Damien were gay. Some of the drawings didn't seem that old. Was there a gay scene in a quiet little backwater like this? It hardly seemed possible but the fact that statistics were offered and telephone numbers were given encouraged him.

But then, he thought more deeply about it. Of course, there are gays everywhere. Why should this place be any different to a city centre pub? He knew he wasn't alone even here. He cleaned the cubicle and washed the backs of the doors but didn't obliterate the drawings. He liked them too much to paint over them and anyway, some of them were quite artistic in fact.

He forgot to tell the others about them. It would be his little secret at least for the time being.

He re-joined the others but he was whistling to himself.

"You sound happy," said Brian, eyeing him carefully.

"I feel happy, young man. This place is going to work for all of us. I can just feel it."

Chapter 5

The opening night arrived in a bit of a blur. Having moved in a few pieces of furniture, the place was habitable and quite comfortable. The living room was still locked. The police had still not completed their investigation but they promised to hurry the proceedings. Word had got out about the opening night.

Graham had kept contact with some army mates and using the internet and mobile phone, he got in touch with guys from his old unit. They promised to show up and get the party going. Steve preferred not to contact any of his old mates but that was understandable because of the circumstances of his departure. He invited Sharon to the opening night but she failed to reply.

She wasn't missed. There were a few of Brian's student friends and they were looking forward to having a good time.

It turned out to be a good mix of army, students and villagers. Steve had organised a disc jockey who arrived early and set his gear up at the far end of the bar. A huge banner over the main door announced that the pub was under new management.

Angie, with a couple of office mates, organised the food. They made chilli con carne with baked potatoes and salad.

The cellar had been restocked and a huge punch bowl was on a central table by the fire. There wasn't really much room to dance but mostly the people were in the mood to drink. It was a cold night in February but everyone received a warm welcome. They all wanted the night to be a huge success…

Graham made a short speech welcoming everyone.

"Before you all get too carried away to care, I would like to say a few words about this enterprise of ours. It wasn't my idea to man a pub, it was this guy's." He indicated to an embarrassed Steve. "Without this guy, this project wouldn't have got off the ground. We wouldn't have found this beautiful old pub in this beautiful county of ours.

"I hope as many of you as possible become regulars here and treat the place as a second home. We already feel at home here. You'll always be welcomed here. We hope eventually to put food on, especially Sunday lunches, but that might have to wait until next year. So bring your kids, wives, girlfriends or boyfriends."

He shot a glance at Steve and a cheer went up. "But the main thing is to enjoy yourselves. So, DJ, let the party begin." The DJ took the cue and launched into the opening number.

A couple of Brian's student friends began to sway together. Angie went off for a cigarette and Graham joined in with a toast to the regiment with his army mates at the bar. The atmosphere was already raucous but good-humoured. About a dozen people had come from the village itself. They had been regular drinkers from Ken and Beryl's days and had come along out of curiosity and also relief that the pub was re-opening.

To tell the truth, the people didn't much care who ran the pub as long as they kept a good pint. So far, they were impressed. The villagers got together by the open fire and watched the girls dancing. They didn't attempt to dance themselves. It was Brian's student friends who kept the party going. They were noisy, excited and drank a lot more than other guests.

Steve wanted all the groups to mingle and he went to sit amongst the villagers. "Are you having a good time?" He asked one middle-aged couple.

"Yes, thank you," said the woman, raising her glass. "Here's to you pals and to you. We hope you make a good go of it."

"Yes, good luck, lads," said her husband. This couple ran the local shop and post office. They were hoping that the pub re-opening might do their business a bit of good.

"We thought it might not be open after that terrible business with Ken," said the wife. "I was a good friend of Beryl. She used to come round for coffee whenever she was in the village. I was always glad to see her. I miss her terribly. We miss both of them obviously. Ken could be a loner sometime; although, I think he was happier in the pub. What do you think, Paul?"

"Oh yes, Ken was happier playing cards in the pub than going to church. He used to keep us amused with his war stories though. He had quite a time of it in Europe."

"They sound like quite a couple. We didn't know them obviously but I hope we can run as good of a business as they did. They ran the place for years, didn't they?"

"Since just after the war finished. Ken was demobbed and they opened the place soon after. Beryl was from the village. She was Llawen born and bred," said Ann.

"Well, I don't promise that we'll make it that long but we hope to stay for a few years," said Steve.

Angie came back and shouted that the food was ready. Everyone had to go in the kitchen and pick it up. It took a good hour to feed everyone. The baked potatoes and chilli con carne went down a treat. They were delicious on a cold winter night.

One lad that Steve noticed didn't go for food. He stayed in his seat. Steve went up to him and asked him why he didn't want any food.

"No thanks, mate. I ate before I came out," he replied. He was good-looking. He was blonde, brown-eyed, and a slightly dark skin; sun tanned probably, thought Steve. When he smiled, his face lit up in an attractive way. A slight hint of a moustache was on his top lip.

He must have been about twenty. He stretched his long legs out in front of the fire and took a drink of whiskey from his glass.

"Did you come with Brian's lot?" Steve asked, expecting him to say he was a student.

"No, I live in the village. My father owns the garage."

"Oh right." Steve was a bit thrown. "What's your name?"

"Sean, Sean Watkins. Pleased to meet you." He held out a hand. Steve took it and enjoyed the firm handshake of the youth.

"I'm Steve," he said.

"I know," said Sean.

Whether it was the heat from the fire or the presence of people but Steve felt a bit uncomfortable. He felt a bit hot. He found it difficult to look away though.

"See you around," said Steve and went to look for food.

He's interesting, he thought to himself. *Hope he stays till the end*. The boy did stay most of the night. He didn't dance or interact much but nursed his glass of whisky by the fire. He seemed happy enough but Steve thought he looked a bit bored. He went up to him again when the party was fully running.

"Are you enjoying yourself?" He asked.

"Yes, it's a good party. I hope you and your friends make a go for it here. We need a bit of life in the village."

"We hope to liven things up a bit. Do you play any sport?"

"We were thinking of starting up a football team. Some of the army lads are meeting to play on Sunday. I don't play much football. I swim and go jogging. Do you jog?"

"I could do if I had someone to jog with. It's a bit boring on your own."

"When do you go?" Steve asked.

"On weekends, any time really. Do you want to call me and arrange a time?"

Steve gave him his number. "You ring me next time you're thinking of going. I'll try and come with you."

"Great," said Sean, putting the number in his wallet. He left the party soon afterwards but Steve didn't see him go.

Shit, I didn't get his number, he thought as the party was breaking up. *I hope he calls*.

The party went on till midnight. The lads were whisked off their feet pulling pints, working the optics, cleaning pint glasses and trying to fathom how to make some of the more exotic cocktails that Brian's student friends ordered. They kept the fire burning as it made the place seem very homely but with all the people present, it soon became very warm and by the end of the night, all the windows were wide open. The heavy strains of *Relax* could be heard around the neighbouring fields.

The sheep turned their heads towards the unaccustomed noise. The final partygoers left around twelve-thirty in the morning in a taxi, noisily slamming the doors and singing good byes to everyone.

The bar was packed but food lay under the tables, cigarettes had been extinguished on the wood, dozens of beer glasses still half-full littered the bar and window sills. It had been a good night.

"Well, how do you think it all went?" Graham asked the next morning as he tackled the dirty glasses.

"I think it went very well. Everyone seemed to be having a good time. I didn't hear many complaints. I enjoyed it," said Steve.

"Yes, I noticed you talking to that young lad. Who is he?"

"His name is Sean and his father owns the garage in the village. He's a quiet lad. I noticed he didn't want to get involved in the chatter much but I do like that sort, quiet and moody," said Steve with a wink.

"Oh yes, he's your sort all right; dark, good-looking, long legs. Any chance of hooking up with him?"

"Maybe. He goes jogging and I've promised I'll go with him next time he goes out. Perhaps Sunday. He's got my number anyway. By the way, do you realise we took over £1200 last night? If it keeps on like that, we'll be millionaires."

"Yes, but it was a special night. People were in the mood to spend. Let's see how much we take on a normal night. It won't be anything like that."

"No, unfortunately. Still, it was a good start. I'll give you a hand with those now."

Washing and drying two hundred glasses takes some time even with a machine to help you and it took over two hours to have all the glasses back gleaming on the shelves again. They restocked the bottles from the cellar and stopped for a coffee. Angie had gone to work feeling a bit hungover and Brian was still in bed.

"Let's get that lazy bastard up," said Steve. "It's gone ten."

"Give him another hour," said Graham. "He did us a favour last night by inviting all his college mates. They were a good crowd, although I noticed a couple of them threw up in the toilet."

"That'll have to be cleaned up before we open at lunchtime."

It was then the police arrived. Graham thought that someone had made a complaint. A sergeant and a young constable came into the bar and asked to speak to the manager.

"We're both managers," said Graham, indicating to Steve. "How can we help you?"

"It's about your previous landlord, Mr Kenneth Smith; the one who shot himself. We're pleased to say that we've finished over enquiries and you can have the keys back to the living room."

The sergeant fished in his pocket and produced two keys which he handed to Graham.

"Great," said Graham. "And did your enquiries reveal anything unusual?"

"In what way?" The sergeant asked, eyeing him carefully.

"Well, is there a problem with his death? It was suicide, yes?"

"Oh yes, it was suicide all right. There's no doubt about that. What we're concerned with was why he committed suicide. He shot himself at night after the pub had closed but we got a phone call from a phone box a few days later to say that something wasn't right at the pub. The milk hadn't been collected and the pub didn't open as usual.

"We had to break in and we found the body of Mr Reece then. We did have a phone call from a young man to say that he knew why Mr Reece had committed suicide but he rang off and never got back in touch. It was a bit of a mystery that one but this shouldn't affect you and your business.

"All of this happened before you became involved in the pub and now that we have concluded our enquiries, you can re-open the room and use it again. The room has been cleaned by our forensic people so there is nothing going on inside. There was quite a bit of blood as you can imagine. There for sure be an inquiry at a later date but we are pretty sure the coroner will confirm our findings."

"Thank you, officers. Poor Ken. I feel sad for him. He survived the war and then ended up like that. Just as well we don't know what is in store for us, eh?"

"Indeed, Sir. Well, we won't take up any more of your time. We can see you're busy. If you need any help with anything, call us but you seem to have everything under control."

The policemen left without having a drink which Steve offered them.

"Well, what do you make of that?" Graham asked.

"I don't know. I'm sure it was just suicide. Maybe someone heard the shot and went to investigate. That person didn't want to get involved so they rang from a phone box to say they had some information about it but then chickened out. I can understand that.

"If the police and coroner were involved, they would have to make a statement or maybe appear in court. That might freak a few people out especially if it was a young person."

"Anyway, let's open the room and take a look."

They were surprised at how neat the room looked. It was a charming sitting room overlooking the car park at the back of the pub. The carpet was missing but the rest of the furniture was in place. A settee and two armchairs took up most of the space but there was a book case full of mostly military books, and a music system with a collection of big band and jazz stacked up against the wall.

Brian would love to have a look at those. The walls had pictures of the pub and some pretty rural scenes on them.

On the fireplace were more pictures of Ken and Beryl at the sea side. One picture had Ken with a monkey on his shoulder photographed on a pier somewhere. There were pictures of foreign holidays with views of the Costa del Sol and Beryl on a beach in one-piece bathing costume eating an ice cream. They seemed happy together. There were no pictures of any children.

"Might be a good idea to re-decorate the whole room, buy new furniture and carpet, and try not to think about what happened," said Steve.

"I agree," said Graham. "No sense in harbouring on the past. We need to move on. It's just a room with a bit of history attached to it that's all; like the story of the hanged lad and the ghost. Don't let it spoil our experience here."

"No, you're right. Even so, I think a complete makeover is on the cards. Leave it to me."

Steve enjoyed spending other people's money. Although the pub had got off to a good start financially, you couldn't really say that they had made any money yet with removal expenses. Even though the pub was up and running with full cellars, they had yet to turn that into a profit. Steve was still broke.

He didn't really have anything worth selling. The car belonged to Graham and after all his years travelling with the army, he hadn't accumulated much by way of material goods. He preferred to travel light. He was the original rolling stone. He should have bought gold in Cyprus.

There were plenty of gold shops in the bazaars, most of them made for the tourist trade but a handsome signet ring with the picture of Wales' feather on it would have been useful. He could have sold it now to raise some much-needed cash. The only other option was to borrow some money. He wondered whether Sean had any.

That Sunday, Sean rang.

"Steve, this is Sean. I'm going jogging this morning if you're interested. I usually go along the river."

"Hi, Sean, I'm glad you rang because I didn't get your number the other night. Yes, I would like to go with you. Where shall I meet you?"

"Well, I'm in the village so say we can meet half-way. The lane that leads to the river could be a good spot. Say in about half an hour."

"Perfect. I'll be there."

And when they met, they were still nervous in each other's company, still fearful of saying the wrong thing. Steve was dressed in his old khaki-coloured fatigues and an old pair of trainers that had seen better days. Sean was dressed in the latest gear of lemon singlet and tight yellow shorts.

His trainers didn't have a speck of dirt on them which Steve found peculiar. Was this man really a jogger? They looked like the dowdy male bird accompanied by the bright flowered female.

They complemented each other.

Sean was waiting for him consulting his new watch every few minutes. They shook hands rather formally and unnecessarily but it was the physical contact which each man needed.

They began to jog down the lane towards the river which was about a mile away.

"I like your gear," said Steve. "It looks new and expensive. I hope you didn't buy it just for me."

"It is new and it cost a fortune but I needed some new running gear. I bought it yesterday in a store in Hereford. The trainers were really cheap but it feels like I'm running on air, they're so light."

"Mine feel like a pair of old army boots. This is the kit we used to wear for physical fitness."

"And very good it looks too," laughed Sean. They were flirting nervously with each other and they ran close together so that occasionally their bodies brushed against one another. The contact thrilled and surprised them. After twenty minutes, they reached the river which was in full flow. They crossed a small bridge and went through a narrow gate that leads to the path along the banks.

The path was originally an old railway line that connected Hereford with Hay. The track had been abandoned thirty years before and nature had partially taken the line. The path followed the river for about a mile and then veered through a series of bends in the river. The boys jogged silently for a while then at a particular deep-end pool bordered by tree, Steve recommended that they take a break.

"How far do you like to jog?" He asked.

"Five miles is enough for me. I might go further mid-week," said the boy.

"Wow, serious stuff," said Steve, impressed.

"It clears my mind and gives me energy," said Sean.

"Energy for what?" Steve asked brazenly.

"Well, I find if I don't go, I get lazy and start to waste my time. I lounge about stay in bed late and loaf about. It drives my parents mad, especially my dad."

They sat on a branch that overlooked the pool and stayed silent for a while. They were so quiet that a pike appeared at the surface of the river swimming against the current but making it look effortless. It put its jaw up to the surface and then disappeared into the depths.

"Haven't seen him before," said Sean. "Did you see those teeth? A vicious creature."

"Sure it goes to show what's lurking below the surface."

Sean looked at him carefully before gazing into the distance.

"Do you think you and your family will stay in this area?" Sean asked.

"We hope to, especially if the pub takes off and we make a few bob; that's really why we came. I haven't settled into anything since leaving the army and I know Graham wasn't happy in his job, so it seemed best. Who knows, we could be here for some time."

They listened to the flow of the river for a while. It calmed them and gave them confidence.

"What about you?" Steve asked. "What do you do? Are you studying?"

"I was," said Sean. "I think I told you my father owns the garage in the village. He had this insane idea that I would take the business over but I know nothing about engines. He even enrolled me to become an apprentice car mechanic last year. What a mistake that was.

"I turned up for the lecture and I couldn't make out what the hell they were talking about. The combustion engine and its workings remained a complete mystery to me. I stuck at it for three months then told him I'd had enough. There was no way I could pass the course without my heart in it. He was disappointed of course but he's got over it."

"My father was a bit like that. He tried to teach me how to drive once. Nearly killed both of us. He thought that by repeating himself, he could make me understand but we learn in different ways. What comes naturally to one is completely alien to others."

"I agree but because of your father, you shouldn't make an extra effort if only to please him. I just wasted quite a lot of my life so I went along with it, but really I should have put my foot down and said no. The day I walked away from that course, I felt as if I had been released from prison after a long jail sentence."

"So how do you spend your time now?"

"I help to do a bit of cleaning in the garage. I take a turn on the till and keep the shelves stocked up. They do allow me to change a tyre now and then. I can do that."

"So what would you like to do seriously?"

"Don't laugh but I really want to be a farmer like my grandad."

"That's a good idea. What kind of farmer?"

"Oh crops and fruits mainly. This is good apple-growing country; the cider makers love the apples from these parts. I noticed you sell local cider in the pub. That's good; you should support local farmers."

"Yes, we do. We sell a few local ciders. My favourite is GX. It's strong but not too sweet. The sweet stuff can get a bit sickly after a while. Well, farmer, eh? I didn't really have you down as the muddy wellies brigade. It takes all sorts. You have to go back to college if you want to be a farmer. There's a lot to learn."

"True. My mother tries to discourage me and says it's too difficult for me. Farming is a hard life but I love being in the open air. I'm enjoying this." He leaned back and stretched his legs out in front of him. He closed his eyes for a minute. Steve scanned his body for the unmistakable sign of a bulge in his shorts. The boy felt relaxed.

Steve swallowed hard. He drank it in. The boy was like a cool glass of cider on a warm day. He wanted to touch him but something held him back. He didn't want to go too fast and maybe make a fool of himself. What if the boy was not interested in him? What if he was just being polite?

"I like you, Sean," he managed to say. "I really like you."

Sean opened his eyes and looked at the ex-soldier boy. He eyed him steadily. "I like you," he said and that was enough for Steve. He put his hand across and felt the bulge. It was visibly growing. He sought permission by looking at the boy. The boy said nothing so consent was tacit.

Steve pulled the shorts down and his semi-erect penis sprang from the cloth. Steve handled him expertly. This wasn't the first time either of them had done this. They trusted in each other's experience not to make it embarrassing or painful. Steve wanted him slowly. The big foreskin still covered the tip and Steve gently forced it back to reveal the head beneath.

"That hurt a bit," said Sean.

"Haven't you pulled the foreskin back yet?" Steve asked genuinely surprised.

"No, it's a bit tight. I have got half back that's all."

"Do you trust me?" Steve asked.

"Yes, go on," said Sean, looking deeply at him.

Steve pressured and massaged the cock gently. Suddenly, the purple head popped out like a rare desert flower that only bloomed once a year and reveals all its glory. Steve pressed it and drew the skin back over the head to make it more comfortable for the boy. Grabbing him lower down the shaft, he freed the spunk up until the boy was writhing in front of him.

"You're a good boy," he said. "You're a good lad. Come on, all of it."

He could sense the boy was close so he cupped his balls in his free hand and jerked him off aggressively. Sean went into a series of shudderings and groanings, and then shot a milky white sperm over Steve's big hand. Steve didn't leave him until the last of the spunk was out and the boy lay prostrate before him.

"Wow, you're a fertile boy," he said ad he wiped the sperm from his hand.

He washed his hand in the river. Sean lay with his shorts around his ankles and his sleepy penis dropping slowly. He awkwardly pulled his shorts up.

"Do you think anyone saw us?" He said gazing around.

"No but who cares? We're both old enough, aren't we? You do have a lovely body, Sean."

"Do you want to come?" Sean asked.

"No, not here. Let's not push our luck. It's enough for me to service you. Make sure you wash your dick tonight behind the foreskin as well. It's important for hygiene."

"I will."

Steve bent down and kissed the lad on the lips. His breath was sweet and tasted of mint. They got up and brushed themselves down.

"We'd better get back," said Steve. "I'll meet you later."

"Promise?" The boy asked.

"I promise," said Steve.

When they parted at the junction, Steve kissed him again to seal their love. They had gone further than either of them really wanted to but the attraction between then was so strong that they couldn't wait. Steve ran all the way back to the pub where he showered and lay on his bed as a drizzle began to fall on the window. He saw it as a lucky sign and could hardly wait for them to meet again.

Chapter 6

Who was this new lad in Steve's life?

Sean's entry into the world had not been an easy one.

He was a large baby and both his parents were in their early forties.

They had both almost given up on the idea of having children. Sean's father, Mr Watkins, ran a successful garage and car repair business in the village. He had married the daughter of the Vicar and they both lived in the house inherited from his father, who had been a farmer. Their lifestyle was comfortable and free from money worries.

The increasing use of cars and the need to service the vehicles meant that business ticked over very nicely and he employed a staff of nine mechanics.

Sean's was a difficult pregnancy. His was also a difficult birth and when he finally arrived at five o'clock in the afternoon, his exhausted mother commented that he looked like a skinned rabbit. She adored him, however, and doted on him. Mr Watkins was pleased that at last, he had a son and heir who might one day take over the business and allow his father to retire early. Sean lacked for nothing; he had the best of everything. His bedroom was full of clothes, toys, and gadgets designed to amuse him. He loved playing with his

Newton's cradle and the model planes and trains fired his imagination.

Something happened, however, at the age of eleven. He suddenly became rather withdrawn and introspective. He stopped playing with his trains and instead went for long walks in the country side with his spaniel. His school work seemed to fall off too.

He always had good reports from school but suddenly, he seemed to be struggling, especially in maths. Sean could do better than the disappointing results from his end-of-year exams noted his math teacher, Mr Struel. His father decided that he needed extra tuition and he attempted this job himself. He was no teacher.

He went too fast and didn't explain in enough detail what was needed. He only succeeded in muddying the water further and confusing the boy. He tried to teach him an attractive way to divide numbers and to work out fractions, but Sean was lost. Sean quickly came to the conclusion that maths was a waste of time. It was an overrated subject.

When was he going to need graphs and simultaneous equations in his day-to-day life? He could see the value of arithmetic but not maths. Arithmetic was useful in the business, especially billing, but that was a luxury he could do without. His father felt disappointed with him.

His GCSE results were mediocre. He excelled in nothing; although his art result was slightly better than the others. His parents wondered what to do with him. They decided that a job in the garage was the best option but he needed to go to college to get some sort of qualification, so they enrolled him on a mechanics course.

Sean lasted three months before informing his father that he was bored and baffled by the course. He swapped courses and tried art. He had slightly more success with that. He could provide a reasonable likeliness to an object but he failed to see that there was a world below the surface of things. He could see no gleam of loyalty in the spaniel's eye.

When asked to analyse a picture by an old master, he just said what he saw. He liked the colours and loved the clothes but could see no point behind the scene. It was just pretty or otherwise.

He was nineteen by now and his only real interest was clothes. His mother spoiled him and bought him whatever he wanted to be dressed up in. He spent a lot of time in front of the mirror. The skinned rabbit had turned into a blonde good-looking lad with a hint of a moustache on his upper lip.

His brown eyes looked a bit sad sometimes and he often had a quizzical look on his face as if he found life a bit of mystery. He didn't make friends at college as others found him a bit odd. He wasn't bullied in any way because he grew up a handsome, tall lad, but he didn't seem to hit it off with anyone. He didn't try to get with any of the girls.

His artwork turned out mundane and a bit boring. He didn't seem to have much imagination.

When it was obvious he wasn't going to advance much at college, his parents withdrew him and his father gave him a job at the garage sweeping up and sometimes helping to change a wheel. Sean hated wearing overalls and getting his hands dirty but the money came in handy to buy clothes. He enjoyed running out in the countryside along the river.

It seemed to calm him down and encourage him to think. His father would have come with him to get to know him better but he always seemed to be too busy.

Sean could jog five miles easily and would often push himself to do more. He was nineteen, fit and eager to prove himself good at something.

Occasionally, he jogged past the pub. Once, when he was jogging, Ken was outside collecting pint glasses from the tables. He called Sean once.

"Looks like you need a drink, lad. Come and have a glass of lemonade or something."

Sean was old enough so he went inside. It was dark inside and it took some time to adjust his vision and after a while, he took it all in. It was summer so there was no fire at the far end. A couple of elderly men were discussing the crops and the price of lambs. They recognised Sean as the son of the garage owner and they engaged him in conversation.

"Been jogging far," said one a farmer that Sean recognised because his father serviced his tractors.

"Five miles so far. I'll do another two today."

"Could be useful, you'll be chasing the women soon," said the other with a wink. "A good-looking lad like you shouldn't have any trouble there."

"They'll be chasing me more like it," said Sean as he downed the lemonade and left. The men laughed.

It wasn't long before he was a regular visitor to the pub. He told his mother he was going for a jog but he would run the half mile or so to the pub and get there by five or six in the evening. He liked to listen to the old men talk or if no one was in, he'd talk to Ken.

Recently Ken lost his wife, Beryl, and she was very much on his mind. They had been deeply in love and their marriage had been a good one; although no children had come along. Beryl was a good landlady. She kept the place spotlessly clean and provided a good Sunday lunch to anyone who wanted it. Pub food was still a bit of a novelty but Beryl and Ken could see which way the business was heading.

Then at the age of sixty, she discovered a lump in one of her breasts. She didn't say anything at first hoping it would go away, but when it didn't, she went to the doctor. Tests were carried out and the doctor concluded it was breast cancer. They were both devastated. Ken remained hopeful that she wouldn't be that ill, she looked so well. Beryl fought it; she even had a breast removed and suffered the chemo.

She remained optimistic. When her hair fell out, she got wigs. When she felt ill, she stayed in bed and Ken nursed her bringing her cups of tea with cake and magazines to help the time go by. At no time did she think she was going to die. The cancer, however, had other ideas. It had spread to the lymph glands and it was only a matter of time.

Ken struggled for a couple of years without her. He missed her terribly. He could still hear her voice in every corner. Sometimes he called back, expecting an answer. He remembered a line from Hardy:

Woman much missed, how you call to me. Call to me.

The only answer was the terrible ticking of the grandfather clock by the fire. It was such a lonely sound. He carried on with his routine. He fetched and cleaned the glasses and put them away. He re-stocked the bottles in the cellar or changed a barrel. He lit the fire in winter and wiped the tables down but his heart wasn't in it.

Somehow the joy had gone out of his life. He began to cut corners and he got lazy. The cobwebs grew, he didn't shave every day, and he took to trying his own beer. So when Sean started to call in, he liked to see the lad.

He talked to him and tried to understand his problems and encourage him to try harder at college or in the garage. Sean liked having him to talk to and took his advice seriously.

Occasionally, Ken would get Sean to stay behind after hours, and with a bottle of whiskey, they'd lock the pub up and retire to the sitting room where Ken would play his jazz records and get the photo albums out. He talked about Beryl mostly.

"You know you remind me of Beryl sometimes," he said.

"Really?" Sean said. "In what way?"

"Oh not the hair, she was a brunette; you're more of a blonde. Your face. When you give that quizzical look about, you remind me as if something was bothering her."

Sean laughed it off.

"I'm not bothered by anything at the moment. Dad scolds me about buying too many clothes and he's always trying to get me to take more interest in his business but I can't seem to see it. A car's a car. It's a means of going from A to B. I don't want to spend my life taking them apart and putting them together again."

"Well, what do you want to do, lad? You'll have to make your mind up some time," said Ken.

"True. I thought I'd like to be a farmer like my grandad but that'll mean going back to college, and it didn't go well for me there. What did you want to do when you were nineteen?"

"Oh, that's easy. We had to join the army. The war had just started and we all had to get involved. I was a lucky soldier though. Did I tell you what happened to me when I was in a troop ship in the channel? Bloody hell, someone was on my shoulder that day."

"What happened?"

"We had just left Pompei a few hours before. We were headed for Brittany and Malo had just been liberated. We could see the French coast in the distance. Some of the boys wanted to play cards. They said we might not have the chance again so we went below and had a game of poker for small change.

"We were enjoying it until this brute of a corporal came down and wanted to join in. He ordered me up on deck so he could sit with the boys and try to win some money. I couldn't argue with him so I left and went back on deck. It was a clear day and visibility was good, and I spotted a plane fast approaching. It was German.

"The pom-poms tried to get him but he was too fast. Anyway, he flew right over the ship and dropped a bomb. By bad luck, it fell right down the funnel and exploded deep in the ship. It killed everyone below. All my mates and that bloody big-headed corporal were killed outright. If I had stayed with them, then that would have been the end of me too.

"I ended up in water for an hour or so and eventually got picked up. I was in a state of shock. That was the nearest I came to being killed in the whole war. It's funny, isn't it, fate?"

"My God, how lucky was that?" Sean said. "Did you ever kill anyone?"

"Plenty of people but you never really saw it close up. They were a target in the distance. But I had to put a badly wounded corporal out of his misery once. I had to use my service pistol. Why was it always me? The others wouldn't do it."

"That must have been hard. Have you still got the gun?" Sean asked, fascinated by his tale.

"Somewhere in the drawer."

Sean got out a heavy standard-issue army pistol. He was surprised at how heavy it was.

"Is it loaded?"

"No, but I do have some bullets for it."

"Didn't you have to hand this in at the end of the war?"

"Yes, but lots of blokes didn't. They kept them and took them home with them. I am glad, I kept mine…"

Chapter 7

Sean and Steve couldn't keep their hands off one another after their initial meeting. Even while Steve was doing a shift behind the bar, Sean would come in, have a drink or two, and then the two would really kiss in the toilet or go behind to the bench in the car park. Neither of them wanted to reveal their love for each other just yet but that moment would come.

They found it sexier to hide their feelings and pretend to be just jogging buddies, which was what everyone thought at first. The only person who thought that there was more going on was Brian. Whether it was intuition or maybe he knew Steve better than Steve thought. He would quiz Sean about the real reason he kept coming to the pub.

Sean knew how to put him off though.

"I'm bored," he would say. "There's not much to do in the village. This is the only place where you can find more entertainment. Why?"

"No reason," said Brian, wiping a few tables. "No reason." He smiled at him and left him alone. But it came out eventually, and what brought it out was the football match. One of the villagers who had attended the opening night thought that it would be a good idea to hold a football match between the army boys, students, and villagers.

It would be a friendly, just to get to know people and they could all return to the pub afterwards to celebrate a win or drown their sorrows. It seemed like a good idea and Graham was keen on it.

"Yes, great idea. Let's draw up a list."

Graham was never happier than when drawing up lists, and on his army side were old mates and new friends that were at the opening night. Steve would play goalie and Brian with a few student friends would play on the villagers' side. The villagers could manage five players including Sean and his college friend, Luke. Sean had been reluctant to play at first but changed his mind when told that Steve would be playing.

The pitch was in the village and there was a very basic changing room available. It was arranged for a Saturday so they could all have a good drink afterwards without worrying about work the next day. Sean, of course, bought an all-new kit. Steve teased him about it.

"This is a village friendly not the FA cup final. Your jogging gear would have been all right."

"Oh no, I want to look the part. I am buying new football boots tomorrow and I expect to see you looking the part too."

"Prepare to be disappointed," said Steve. "I can't afford new gear like that."

"You're like Ken," said Sean.

"Ken who used to run this place. He was tight with money? How do you know?"

"Well, I used to come here before you lot showed up on the scene. He was well known for being tight with money. That's how the fire started upstairs. Rather than putting the dryer on, he'd put clothes in front of the electric fire. They

105

caught fire one night as he dozed off and burned the bedroom."

"Oh, right," said Steve and left it at that, but he was left with the nagging suspicion that Sean knew Ken better than he was letting on.

The Saturday of the match, it was raining slightly. The windows of the pub had steamed up and Steve wiped them with a cloth and gazed out to the field opposite. He was looking forward to the match and he wasn't going to be put off by a bit of rain. He had even bought a small cup to give to the winning team.

Brian thought that he was taking the match too seriously, but could see that it was good for relations between the pub and the villagers and could increase trade.

"Have you played goalie before?" Brian asked just before they were off.

"Oh, yes. I always played a goalie in the army. I'm quite good I'll have you know."

"Well, we'll see how good you are later," said Brian.

"What position are you going to play in? You'd better not move against us that could be embarrassing."

"Don't worry, I don't think there's much chance of that. Most of my mates reckon, I've got two left. I was never much good at sports in school. I used to avoid feet PE any way I could get away with it. Later in the 6th form though, I got into tennis and squash. I found that I could handle a racket better than kicking a ball. I do have a competitive streak in me though. I don't like to lose."

"Well, don't be too competitive this afternoon. It's meant to be friendly, don't forget," said Steve.

"Will your mate Sean be playing?" Brian asked.

"I suppose so. He is part of the village team. He's fit and can run fast," said Steve.

"But you can catch him, eh? Oh, I forgot, you'll be in goal. Well, you'll have to admire the boy wonder from afar," laughed Brian.

"Twat," was the only answer.

They got to the village in Graham's car about a quarter to twelve.

Most of the players had arrived, changed and were milling around, stretching limbs, and moving amongst themselves.

"Oh, you finally managed to make it then," quipped Simon, one of Graham's friends.

"George said that he might be late, he had a dental appointment this morning but he said he wouldn't miss it for the world."

Steve went over to talk to Sean who was passing the ball to another youth.

"Are you all right?" He asked.

"Yes. This is Luke, an old school friend of mine. He lives in the next village but I didn't think anyone would mind."

Luke raised his hand to say hello. The two lads carried on passing the ball and Steve went to change. The changing room was cramped and a bit smelly. Generations of cricketers and footballers had used them and although, there were showers, there weren't enough of them and many of the lads preferred to wait until they got home.

That particular mixture of sweat and heat as well as the pungent embrocations used to relieve muscle pain caused a smell that was impossible to remove, even with all the windows open.

The referee was a local primary school teacher who normally refereed football matches but she knew enough of the rules to cope with a football match. Each team member wore a tabard either red or yellow and a couple of villagers were well into their thirties. They were referred to as grandad on the pitch. You are allowed to shoulder tag in football, otherwise it's meant to be a no-contact charge.

Strangely though, there seemed to be a lot of contact taking place that day. The poor referee seemed to blow up every five minutes in the first half for infringements of rules. Sean's mate, Luke, was particularly aggressive with a couple of army lads, ending up on the floor clutching their ankles or hands.

"Send him off, ref," was a cry that went up four-five times during the first half. The other players began wary of tackling him, so much so that he was allowed too much freedom to play and he scored the only goal in the first half.

During the interval when oranges were passed around, the army boys went into a huddle to discuss the best way to deal with him. It must have worked because soon after the start of the second-half, Luke was trapped between two army players who charged him from both sides. He went down like a pole hit by a bull and stayed on the ground. The players gathered around and looked concerned.

"That was a bit tough, lads," said Graham, genuinely concerned for the boy groaning on the ground. "It's only supposed to be a bit of fun."

"Sorry, Graham," said one of the culprits. "We did go in a bit hard. Are you all right?"

"I'll go off for a bit," said Luke, limping to the side of the pitch. He watched the rest of the game from the side-lines, offering vocal support whenever he could. His ankles were swollen up like a cricket ball. Being one man down made a big difference to the village team.

The pub and army side scored two goals in quick succession and stayed 2-1 up for the rest of the match. The chaotic nature of the game didn't seem to distract from the pleasure generated indeed the wild chases after the ball had all the thrill of a fox hunt.

The ball became the fox passed in a haphazard way by horses and hounds. Collisions occurred resulting from an excess of zeal rather than malevolence. The men became sweaty and breathless were caught up in the pursuit.

They kept it going until the full ninety minutes. The amateurs played more with enthusiasm than with skill, and when an exhausted referee blew the final whistle, everyone thought it had been a good match and that the correct score prevailed in the end. A lot of cheers, back-slapping and shaking of hands followed and they wanted to do it again sometime.

The lads went back to the changing room and began to exchange stories about what just happened.

"Did you see that header of mine," said Mike, one of the army boys.

"Yes, a real Geoff Hunt you are," said Graham, whipping him with a towel.

"Not half as good as that pass I made to Steve to set up that final goal," boasted Nigel. "Over the defender's head and landed right at his feet. Good goal. I didn't think normally that was a good pass but I couldn't really miss from there, could I?"

The men showered in turn and dressed themselves on the porch. A little group of admiring girls from the village eyed the lads, nervously giggling to themselves every now and then. The army boys loved it and showed off their muscles and tattooed arms to the girls.

"What do you think, girls? Good game or what?" Ryan shouted, a particularly fine specimen of a jock was the lad.

The girl just laughed and looked away. Steve was quiet and a bit subdued, outplayed by the other's boldness. "Are we on now for a pint at the pub?" Nigel asked.

"We most certainly are," said Graham. "First one's on the house. Thanks for supporting us, we appreciate it. There'll be sausage and chips for those who want it."

A big cheer followed that announcement. They had all worked up an appetite and thirst. They gathered up their kits and started going their way to their cars. Sean caught up with Steve as he combed his hair in the mirror.

"That went well," he addressed the reflection.

"Yes, I'm really pleased and thank you for playing. You were great."

"Oh, get out. I hardly touched the ball," said Sean.

"You did. You had a couple of good passes I noticed. You look stunning in that kit by the way." He lowered his voice so the others couldn't hear.

"Do you think so," said Sean. "You didn't look so bad yourself. The army lads are fit. I suppose there's plenty of chance to play in the army and that keeps one fit. Anyway, there are some good-looking lads here too," he said, grinning at the horse play going on around him.

"Yeah, it's sometimes difficult to keep your eyes on the job," said Steve, looking at Ryan pulling on his jeans.

"Yeah, he's gorgeous. Available?" Sean said wisely.

"Certainly not, and stop being a tart. You've found your solider boy, you're looking at him," he said.

"So I have," said Sean, and picked up his training kit. "See you at the pub in a few minutes."

They still wanted to go through the charade of arriving and leaving separately, so it was twenty minutes before Sean arrived back at the pub. He had walked and jogged here from the playing field and had come via the brook at the back of the pub.

"I thought you had changed your mind," said Steve as he saw Sean walk through the door.

"As if," he answered. "My usual please, barman."

"That'll be a lemonade then, with a twist," said Steve, pulling him a pint of lager.

The bar was already lively. The food hadn't arrived yet but was on its way. Stuart was telling everyone what a great goal he had scored and everyone agreed with him. Sean got his pint and made his way to the fire and his usual seat, only to find Ryan there ahead of him. He had his legs outstretched.

He looked the epitome of male self-satisfaction and he smiled as Sean approached. He undressed the boy with his eyes and made room for him on the settle.

"Room for a little one," he said.

"Oh, you've seen me before then," said Sean.

"Only joking. You're Steve's mate, yeah?"

"Yes, he's a mate of mine. You had a good game today."

"Not bad, I enjoyed it. It was a good workout. What about you? Do you enjoy a good workout, eh?"

"Are we still talking about football?" Sean asked, looking him fully in the face.

"Of course."

Ryan pulled his long legs in, allowing Sean to sit next to him.

Their legs rubbed against each other. The electricity shot up Sean's spine.

"How long have you and Steve been friends?"

"Oh, a couple of months now. What about you? Do you have a good friend?"

"Used to but I'm a free agent now. I wouldn't mind getting back in the saddle though. I'm getting horny now," he said boldly.

"Wow, you don't mess around. Are you bi?" Sean asked.

"Something like that." The fire seemed to make the two hot and they shuffled awkwardly in the seat. Sean looked over to Steve who was busy working behind the bar. He probably wouldn't notice if he was absent for a while.

Temptation was too much for him.

"Meet me around the back," said Ryan. Sean said nothing but watched the good-looking lad go to the toilet at the back. Sean knew he shouldn't go but he just couldn't resist it. He gave Ryan five minutes then got up to go the toilet.

The bar was full and nobody noticed him go.

Ryan stood at the urinal displaying his manhood; it was erect and excited.

"We're taking a risk," said Sean standing next to him.

"No problem. We're two big boys. Now just show me your cock."

Sean unzipped and pulled his swollen member out. Ryan was impressed.

"Let me wank you," he said, and he got behind the boy and grasped him firmly. He wanked him hard for five minutes.

He had a good grip on. The boy started to writhe and moan. He couldn't hold it in so he shot into the urinal and steadied himself with a hand on the wall. Ryan stopped.

"Good boy," and he put his cock away.

"Don't you want to come?" Sean asked.

"No, it takes a long-time for me to come. I'll see you again soon. We'd better go back or we'll be missed."

They had only been gone for ten minutes but Steve had noticed they were missing. He was disappointed a bit when he realised they had gone out together but the bar was busy and he couldn't leave Graham on his own. So, he carried on serving. He looked at Sean as they entered the room but Sean avoided his gaze. They had lost their seat and had to stand. They looked for a table together.

The encounter had come out of the blue and had lasted barely ten minutes but Sean knew he had made a problem for both of them. Would Ryan keep his mouth shut or would their secret be out? Should he just come clean and admit to a quickie?

It didn't say much for the relationship if at the arrival of the first good-looking man he would give himself to him so easily. He felt like a scrubber. The trouble was that of his sex urge and he had to accept that.

But it wasn't going to be easy. Sean decided to go home but as he was making his way to the door, Steve caught his arm and led him to the sitting room.

"Why are you leaving? I thought you were going to stay for something to eat." Steve looked at the boy closely.

"I was but I'm not really that hungry now, and you hurt my wrist just then."

"Sorry, I didn't mean to. Are you all right? You look a bit flushed."

Sean sat down on the settee and looked at his hand in his lap.

"Something happened out the back with Ryan," he said, his voice thickening as he said it. Honesty was probably the best policy.

"I thought so. Wait till I get my hand on him, I'll give him a thick lip."

"No, don't do that, please. You'll embarrass me. It was my fault. It was my idea, he just changed his mind. We haven't told anyone, after all, he didn't know."

"No, but you did. Why did you go with him? What did you do? Did he fuck you? Don't tell me you did that!"

Steve was getting a bit worked up and Sean had to calm him.

"No of course not, calm down. I'm not a virgin anyway you know that. I've been with other men I told you. I've always been honest with you, Steve." He looked up at him and smiled weakly.

"Yes, you said it was a while ago when you were a schoolboy. You said you were expecting that but you didn't know that you really wanted that. Once or twice you had but that you regretted it afterwards, that's why I haven't asked you to do it with me."

"I want to wait until we were both sure that's what we want. Are you saying it's not me you want to be with? You prefer Ryan?"

"No, don't be silly. That was me and the alcohol and the fire and long legs. He caught me off guard. I wouldn't normally do that. I like you too much for that."

"So why go with him if it's me you want?" Steve was getting emotional now. He thought that Sean was one.

"I don't know really. It's kind of wanting to humiliate myself with other men. I might have low self-esteem that's why I keep buying new things. It's a way of making me feel good about myself. Sometimes I want to punish myself for what I've done. I think maybe I'm a bad person. Oh, help me, Steve."

He began to sob on the sofa, and for the first time, the mask slipped and he looked like the lost and lonely boy that he was. Steve put out his arm around him and comforted him, and eventually, the sobbing stopped.

"You're going to have explain a bit more. I don't understand. Are you saying you're done something illegal?"

"Not really, just unsure." He looked around the room. "I hate this fucking room," he said. "Ken used to bring me here. We did it once on this very sofa."

"What? You and Ken had sex? When?"

"About six months before he shot himself. He wanted me and kissed me. I let him do it. He was lonely after Beryl died and he still had the sex urge. Although he was finding it hard to get a full erection, I was patient with him. I told him he was still a good-looking guy, although he was already seventy by then. I told him he could still marry again.

"He gave me drinks and money sometimes. I told him I wanted to buy things like trainers and expensive jeans just to impress my school friends. He said he'd look after me and he did."

"Oh, for fuck's sake, he was your sugar daddy? The dirty old sod. How old were you then?"

"Last year at school. Seventeen or so. I knew I was leaving soon so I thought 'what the hell'. He used to keep saying I looked a bit like Beryl. He gave me a few bob and he'd keep his mouth shut, so why not?"

"Yes, but why not is because you were still in school. What if your parents had found out? They'd have been devastated. How much did you rock him for?"

"Don't say it like that, it sounds awful. But I did begin to get greedy. He became a bit strange. He wanted me to dress up for him; not in women's clothes but in sports gear; once in leather. I didn't mind giving him pleasure but I started asking for more money. It became like a drug. He said he loved me and I said the same back but of course, that wasn't between us and…"

Just then, Graham appeared at the door.

"Everything all right here, buddy?" He asked Steve. "It's getting a bit busy out here with the food and all and we need your help."

"Ok, mate. I'll be there now. I think we're about done here anyway."

Graham disappeared and Steve turned to Sean, who was still subdued.

"Well, I don't know what to say. I'm speechless. I thought I knew you a bit but I don't know you at all. You've been acting like a rent boy and I've had bitter experiences of them in the past honestly. Sean, I don't know what to make of it. My head is all over the place. I've got to get back to work now. I'll ring you later. Are you still going home?"

"Yes, I think I'd better, don't you? Please don't judge me too harshly. I'm young and made a mistake but I'm not a bad lad at heart and I do really like you, you know that."

They said bye and parted. Steve needed to think about this one. The boy's story had completely thrown him. He knew Sean had had sex with other boys and men, but a seventy year old. What was he thinking of? And did Sean have anything to do with Ken's death? That was an unwelcome thought that really worried him.

Best to keep his head down and stay busy. They needed to make money from the business and not get involved in dodgy love affairs. He ignored Sean's calls for a while.

Chapter 8
The River

Whenever Steve was in trouble, he turned to the river for strength and guidance. *The Adventures of Huckleberry Finn* was his favourite book. He did not read much now but he loved that book with a passion that was hard to explain. The sheer romance of the river caught him. The not knowing what was around the next bend appealed to his adventurous nature.

The voyage of the raft down the wide river, a runaway slave and a young adventurous lad appealed to the rebel in him. So, a week after learning more about Sean, he contacted him and suggested that they canoe down the river to a small island that lay on a bend.

It was covered in trees,but you could land on it and take a picnic into the middle of it. It seemed a perfect idea to get to know more about the enigmatic lad he had taken up with. Sean was delighted with the plan. The two men could come here, take a picnic, drink beers maybe and do some swimming. It should be idyllic.

The canoe had to be delivered close to where they had been jogging and to be picked up a couple of miles farther downtown because neither of them wanted to paddle upstream against a strong current.

On Sunday, it was a grey day but not raining. The delivery man had already unloaded the canoe and it lay on the bankside like a beached porpoise. Steve had done a lot of canoeing in the army and as a result, he could handle it.

"Have either of you canoed before?" The delivery man asked, who had driven all the way from Hereford.

"Yes, in the army I've done canoeing, cycling and running. I'm confident I can handle this."

"And you can both swim?"

"Yes, we're good swimmers," said Sean helping to get the boat in the river.

"Okay, have a good time. I'll pick the boat up at Broden bridge around five o'clock. If for some reason you can't make it, please give me a ring in good time to save me a journey. We can make alternative arrangements."

"No worries, we'll make it. We've got life jackets, paddles and canoe, we're sorted. See you later," said Steve, impatient to climb in first in front.

"I'll steady her, you climb in. Put the picnic gear in the front."

When Sean was safely ensconced, he passed the basket to Sean to tie it at the front of the boat. With the help of the delivery man, Steve got in and they were soon away. They waved to the man as the river took them away quite quickly; more quickly than Sean had anticipated.

The river was flowing fast and deep. They both preferred to stay close to the bank at first but as their confidence grew and they learned the ways of the boat, they started to move towards the centre of the river. They pulled slowly. The island was a good mile away downstream but at this rate, they would make it in half an hour.

They were both too busy for a few minutes to appreciate the scenery around them but the mixture of trees along the bank were impressive. They were just beginning to come into leaf. The hint of green could just be made out among the grey and brown.

The Wye is an impressive river during the whole year but in spring, it is beautiful. The 'Sylvan' Wye as Wordsworth called it, learned it, wound its long way through the county calling at various town and Hereford of course.

The fishing is good and the signs of pollution are small. The boys soon got used to the rhythm of the boat as it rocked them like babies in a pram.

"This is great, Steve," said Sean.

"You don't have to shout, I'm right behind you."

"Sorry, I'm just so excited. This is my first time in a canoe. I've always wanted to go out on the river but I felt a bit scared on my own. Thank you for inviting me."

"No problem, just keep an eye out for rocks. We want to avoid them if possible. Steer for the deeper part of the river."

"Look, that's Burton farm over there. We receive their vehicles." A fine, old stone home came into view. It was some way from the river and had a field between it and the river. It was a farm that he seemed to know well but he had never seen it from this angle before.

A couple of sheep dogs barked at them near the edge, one even came to the water's edge but quickly went back again. To flow was too fast for it.

"If that's Burton farm, it means the island is only about half a mile away," said Sean, still too loudly.

"Got that," laughed Steve. He deliberately splashed the boy from behind. They were both enjoying then. It got tricky as they approached Barton Bridge and they had to steer through the middle arch which was not that wide. A tractor crossed over as they went under the bridge.

"You can slow the canoe down by trailing the paddle through the water, let's practice," said Steve.

"We don't want to go straight past it when we come to it."

"No chance of that," said Sean, practicing the man oeuvre.

When the little island came into view, they could see that the undergrowth had been cleared away to make it easier for boats to approach the island.

"You stay in the boat," said Steve. "Let me get out and steady her. I'll try not to rock her too much." Sean grabbed a handful of outgrowing branches and brought the boat to a halt. Steve got out and pulled the boat towards the landing place. The water was about a foot deep here and he skilfully tied the boat up to a post positioned nearby.

It was firmly anchored. Sean handed him the picnic and then got out himself. Neither man really weighed too much so the rocking of the boat was minimal. It bobbed and rocked with the water. It seemed alive, almost anxious to resume its journey but prevented by a stray rope. It was tied on a firm leash, anxious to bind away if the owner would let it.

It was mid-day and the weak sun reflected on the bouncing water. Sean carried the basket through the undergrowth and soon trees revealed a dry spot in the middle of the island. They were surrounded by vegetation here and would not be seen by anyone walking along the river bank. Like Huckleberry they pulled the leaves apart to spy on what was happening on the bank. No one was around. "It's private," said Sean. "No one can see us here. We're completely alone."

"Just how I want you," said Steve and kissed him on the mouth.

"Shouldn't we eat first?" Sean said.

"Are you hungry?" Steve asked pulling away from him.

"Not really," said the younger boy. He got a plastic sheet out of the bag and spread it on the floor.

"Can we strip off?" Sean asked doubtfully.

"Why not, no one can see in here. Let me have a good look at my lovely boy," he said greedily.

They quickly stripped. Both men were aroused and Sean playfully got behind the older man, grabbed his cock, and began to masturbate him eagerly.

"You like to dish it out, don't you? Now learn to take it," he said as he cupped Steve's balls in one hand and wanked him with the other. Steve let him do it for a few minutes until his cock was very hard. Then, he turned the tables and set the boy to the ground. They both fell on the sheet laid out before them.

They had not had full sex until this minute but now was the time. Lubricating his cock with gel brought especially for this. He inserted a finger into the boy's ass. It was tight and resisting.

"Relax, I won't hurt you," he said urgently.

"I'm trying," said Sean, feeling the foreign finger probe it. After a while, he relaxed and the finger did its job.

"There you go," said Steve. He lubricated the boy expertly and Sean began to moan. He felt he was in the hand of an expert and he trusted him. Steve put him on all fours. He took out his finger and put gel on his cock. It felt like poker in his hands.

He was pleased with the way it felt. He waited to please the boy and this was his way of doing it. It felt right to both men; it didn't feel unnatural or strange.

"Relax now," said Steve. The tip of the penis was in the anus and beginning to work its magic. To feel a foreign body enter your own is alarming but thrilling. It's an experience only men will really know. They sacrifice so much by being gay but now, it was payback time. The boy took half of the member. The older man began to thrust and began to get right up in it. He went too far.

"You've been a naughty boy. You've been with that Ryan and now I'm going to punish you," he said.

Sean looked around to see if he was joking but the older man was completely dominating him now and he looked serious. He pushed the penis right in and then hard. It hurt the boy a little and he yelped but the feeling of complete domination excited him so much that he suffered the pain. Steve thrust and thrust again until he felt the sperm shoot out in relief. He lay on top of the boy still deep inside him.

The birds and the animals of the island from the hidden places saw the copulating men. They must have been confused to see some strange new creature in their kingdom. They had never seen one before that didn't seem to require a female.

Sean didn't move; he felt sore and wanted to get comfortable.

"You're hurting me, get off." It was a relief when Steve withdrew.

"Fucking hell," he said. "What was all that about? You want to punish me. What for?" He began to pull up his shorts.

"Sorry, I got carried away. Did I hurt you?"

"A bit, yes. That's not a piece of meat you know. He sounded hurt."

"I know. Sorry, Sean. I do love you, you know," he said apologetically.

"I hope you don't do it like that every time," he said. "I don't think I could take it."

"No, I was nervous and horny as hell. I wanted to impress you," he said sheepishly. He gazed down at his diminishing penis and felt ashamed.

Sean put his arms around him. "Hey, it's ok. Still love you, big stud. Next time, leave out the punishment bit, that's all. I can take you. I am big enough but it's supposed to be a thrill for both of us, not just the one on top. Do you always fuck like that?"

"It helps. I come very quickly if I play-act. I like to feel in complete control. That's what happened with that boy in Cyprus, the one that cost me my job in the army. I was fucking him on the beach and got carried away, like I did with you. He was telling me to stop and pull out but I carried on fucking him hard until I came. He complained about me to get his own back I suppose. I don't really blame him. I must have hurt him a bit."

"That makes sense now. You've got a problem with this, haven't you? If I am not the first one you've gone and punished in this way, it means there is a pattern to it. We'll have a discussion about this later when we've calmed down a bit."

Sean was being the sensible one, the bigger man. Steve was confused and a bit embarrassed. He couldn't look him in the eye. They ate their picnic in silence.

Finally, Sean spoke. "Actually, now that we're being honest with each other, I've got a bit of a confession to make."

"Oh," said Steve, expecting another Ryan.

"Yes, you know when I said that Ken didn't have to try to dress me up as a woman, that wasn't really true."

"I thought there was more to that particular story," said Steve. "Mind you, I think you would make a great woman."

"Shut up and listen. He had been pestering me to dress up for him for a while. Usually, it was in sports gear or swim wear. He even bought me a pair of leather trousers once. I liked them too. I've still got them."

"But this is about something else."

"Yes, one night, he showed me a picture of Beryl when she was a young woman. He was proud of that picture. They had been on a picnic by the river and she was lying on the grass laughing and smiling. They were happy together. She was a good-looking woman.

"Beryl had long, curly brown hair in the style of those days, quite natural. She wore a white blouse and sandals. The skirt was certainly quite attractive. The picture was special to Ken and he had taken it with him when he went away to war. It had probably been half-way around Europe in his wallet.

"Anyway, he showed it to me one night. We both had a few to drink. Ken was drinking more and more in those days."

"Would you do something for me, Sean?" He said.

"What?" I said.

"Would you dress up like Beryl? One time; just one time? You look a bit like her when she was young and it would be like having her with me once again."

"I honestly didn't know what to do or say. It obviously meant a lot to him and I felt it would be mean not to do it, so I did."

"You dressed up as Beryl," said Steve. "Now I wasn't expecting that. Where did you get her clothes from?"

"From her wardrobe upstairs. She still had the blouse and skirt, although I couldn't find the sandals so I was barefoot. I put her skirt on and her blouse. They fitted quite well. I padded the blouse up a bit with a couple of stockings. I put on some makeup, but not too much. I didn't want to make her look like a tart. She was the love of his life and all."

"But what about her hair? You've got totally different hair. Hers was more of a dark brown, almost black."

"Yeah, that was the really weird bit. I came across some wigs that she had worn when having her cancer treatment. She had lost her hair by then and she had chosen wigs that reminded her of when she was young. They were long and curly. I chose one and put it on.

"When I looked at myself in the mirror, I was shocked. There was Beryl staring back at me. It was as if all the years had melted away and she was eighteen again. It was unnerving."

Sean stopped for a while and took a drink. Steve didn't press him and let him carry on in his own time.

"So, I went downstairs to see Ken. He was on the settee drinking whisky. I had the strange feeling that I might have made a mistake dressing up as her."

"He went crazy with you?" Steve asked.

"No, he started to cry. He dropped the whisky glass and just stared at me crying all the while."

"Oh, I'm sorry, Ken," I said. "I didn't want to upset you. I'll take it off."

"No," he said. "You're beautiful. You look just like her. You've brought my lovely Beryl back to me," he said getting close to me. He kissed me on the lips and talked to me. He started calling me Beryl and saying how much he loved and missed me. His breath stank of whiskey. The bloody wig fell off and it seemed to break the spell.

"Get out, get out," he shouted. "You're not my Beryl, you're just a greedy rent boy. Go on, fuck off."

"He was starting to get nasty at this point so I thought I'd better get out from there. I escaped wearing the gear. I told my parents I had been to a fancy dress party and had come home early. It was a day later that I heard he had shot himself with his army revolver. Don't you see; it was me that made him do it.

"Dressing up like that brought it all back to him and I suppose he couldn't live without her anymore. I made him kill himself."

"No, whoa! You didn't pull the trigger, he did that," said Steve.

"It was as good as pulling it. When I left him, he was upset and drunk. They said that when they found him slumped on the settee, there was an open photograph album next to him all spattered with blood. I had brought back the past and it was too much for him. Oh, Steve, I feel miserable about it." Sean began to sob.

"Listen to me, you. What you did, you did out of charity to that old man. He asked you to dress up and to please him and you did. Unfortunately, the likeness was just a bit too much for him, and in his drunken state for a short while, he honestly did think you were Beryl.

"You have nothing to feel bad about. You wanted to please a sad and lonely old man. You couldn't have known how it was going to work out. Stop blaming yourself." He put a protective arm around the sobbing youth and rocked him gently. They stayed like that for twenty minutes, just holding on to one another. Each was reluctant to break the spell but eventually, Steve pulled away and said they'd better get back. They had to return the canoe by five o'clock and they had to paddle another couple of miles.

They packed up quickly and were ready to return home. It had been an exhausting day and they needed to rest. When they reached the bridge, the owner was waiting for them. He helped them to drag it out of the water.

"How did you get on? It's a great little boat, isn't it?"

They said yes, it was great, and left it at that. He sensed there was something wrong but put it down to tiredness. It could really take it out of you to paddle one of these things for the afternoon. They loaded the canoe on to the trailer and got into the back of the 4x4.

Neither of them said much on the way home. Desperately, the driver tried to make conversation and they promised to keep in touch also. Both needed time to process what they had learned about the other that afternoon.

Chapter 9

Steve and Sean lay low for a few days. Steve concentrated on the pub. The business was going well. They had built up a regular trade. Market day on a Wednesday was the busiest during the week. Farmers who had made good money selling their livestock at Hereford market called in at the pub on their way home, to celebrate a good deal.

They often drank whisky which made for healthy profit. The farmers liked the homely feel of the place. The fire at the far end, the comfortable settee and the trinkets lovingly polished by the boys decorating the shelves. If the customers wanted privacy, they could drink with their friends in one of three booths placed on one side of the bar.

Here they could lower their visits and hold a private conversation out of hearing range of the noisy rancour at the bar. The talk generally tended to be about farming and the difficulties of making a profit, especially during the recession, but profits were being made and none of them were spent at the pub. Graham, in particular, was good at conversing with the customers.

"Had a good day, gentleman?" He would enquire a group of farmers drinking in one of the booths.

"Yes, very good. Just got 86 pound a head for a flock of Welsh mountain lambs. The price is high at the moment. Have a drink on us, mate."

"Thank you, I'll just take a half with you. Whereabouts do you come from?"

"Over at Llangower, near Hay. I've got three hundred acres of land. Jim is my neighbour, he's got five hundred acres."

"More area just means more hassle," said Jim modestly.

"I must admit," said Graham, "the price of lamb is high. I can't remember the last time we had a good lamb dinner. We tend to eat more chicken. Why is the price so high?"

"Well, the supermarket doesn't help. They demand good quality and that means more expense for us. You can't feed them lame old stuff, it has to be the top-grade stuff and that can be expensive."

"It's daylight robbery what they're charging for food these days," said Jim, morosely. "Add on to that what we lose when it's a bad winter, plus what we can lose with sheep rustlers. That can be a major problem. People coming up in the middle of the night and just loading them onto trailers.

"Some of them even have their own dogs, would you believe? It's a growing problem too; there's going to be more of it."

"Did you know that this place is haunted?" Graham said.

The men looked interested. "You talking about sheep stealing reminded me of the young lad who was hanged here for stealing sheep back in the 1650s. He was brought here by the magistrates, found guilty and hanged. He was only fourteen. We've had his ghost here ever since. It appears on a harvest moon night so they say. It walks along the corridor upstairs."

"Dew, dew," said the farmer. "Aren't you scared of sharing your house with a ghost? You could get the vicar to do an exorcism."

"No," said Graham. "I quite like the idea of sleeping with a ghost. It gives the place some character. None of us has seen anything but we haven't seen a harvest moon yet. That's around September time. We've got a few months to go yet."

A well-built middle-aged man entered the bar and asked to see Steve. Steve was busy in the kitchen preparing sandwiches for the farmers. He came out still wearing his apron.

"Hello, you want to see me?" He asked.

"Yes, my name is Nigel Watkins, I'm Sean's father. I want a word with you about my son, Sean."

By his tone of voice, Steve could tell he was angry, so he ushered him into the sitting room for a private conversation.

Mr Watkins sat on the settee and addressed him.

"I gather you've been seeing rather a lot of my son. He's upset about something. He hasn't eaten properly for days. Nor slept and I think it's got something to do with you. Are you having some kind of sexual relationship with my boy?" Mr Watkins looked him straight in the face. Steve shuffled on the spot in front of him.

"Why? What has Sean said?"

"No matter what he said. Answer my question. Have you had sex with him?"

"We like each other. We've been seeing each other."

He couldn't say the 's' word.

"I see," said his father. "I want you to stop seeing him. You're confusing him and making him miserable, can't you see that? He's easily swayed, always has been and you've putting ideas into his head that will lead him astray. He's a very impressionable lad and you're quite a bit older than him. I and his mother only want him to be happy. He's always been a sensitive lad and there was some trouble at school once with a teacher. We sorted that out and insisted he changed school. We've been careful to protect him."

"I didn't know. He didn't tell me that," said Steve. "He is twenty-one Mr Watkins. He's not a teenager He's a grown man. Surely he should know his own mind by now?"

"He's more like a child. He's our only son and we want to protect him so we think it would be better all around if you stopped seeing him. We've told him he's not to come here again or try to communicate with you in any way. Please don't try to get in touch with him. It'll be hard for him but he must stop. Please co-operate with us and stop this obsession from developing any further."

"It's not an obsession, I love the boy and I think he loves me. If you want to make him happy let me see and have a word with him in private. I'll try to find out what's wrong."

"No, leave him alone, Let me and his mother deal with him. We know him better than you do, after all. Are you a married man?" he asked with some concern in his voice.

"No," said Steve and lowered his eyes.

"I thought not. He's not the right person for you, please leave him alone."

Steve could hardly argue with that. He saw Mr Watkins out. His head was in turmoil now. *What the hell had Sean told them? Had he said anything about what had happened on the island? Perhaps he said he'd been raped.* He regretted being so rough with the lad; if only he had been a bit gentle with him.

Until he talked to Sean, he wouldn't know what had happened. He guaranteed that it was more to do with Ken and the suicide than him.

Things went quiet for a week then development took a strong turn. It was late on a Wednesday night. Trade had been slow and the boys were beginning to count up and clean the bar.

Suddenly, a taxi turned up outside and Sean stepped out, coming with a suitcase and a hold-all. He had a scarf around his face and looked as if he had been crying. He went straight to the bar where Steve was washing glasses.

"Sean, where have you just come from?"

"Steve, can we go somewhere quiet and talk?"

"Sure, come into the sitting room. Graham, can you manage without me for a bit?"

"Yes, but help me clean the floor later on, will you?"

"Sure. Come into the room, Sean."

They went into the sitting room and sat down facing one another.

"I had your father here the other day. He said that he and your mother were worried about you. What's going on?"

"They want me to stop seeing you but I don't want to do that. You've been the best thing that's ever happened to me. They think I'm obsessed with you but it's love, not obsession. They can't recognise the difference."

"They can but they don't want to. So, what are we to do about it?"

"I want to move in here with you. Please say yes. I can't live at home any more. They treat me with suspicion all the time. My father even took my mobile phone off me."

"Yes, that is a punishment. Send you off to bed with no supper?"

"Exactly, it's ridiculous. I'm twenty-one for God's sake."

"But if you lived here, and I'm not saying you can't because we have plenty of room here, won't it make things worse?"

"How can it get much worse?"

"Point taken. But what will you do all day? You're not going to college, you don't have a job. You probably don't have much money now…"

"I've no money," Sean corrected him.

"Right, so, I'll have to support you for a while until you get on your feet. With my money worries, I didn't think I would hear myself saying that. It won't be easy but I have saved up a bit in the last few months. The pub is doing ok. You could help with the cleaning and stocking of the shelves. Actually, Brian might be grateful for someone of his own age to play with."

"Yes, I get on with Brian. I could be his assistant. It would probably only be for a few weeks until I get organised. What do you think?"

"What about your stuff? You haven't brought much with you."

"True. I had to take advantage of them both being out at the same time. Wednesday is my mother's bridge night and dad is meeting a friend of his in town. I threw a few things into a suitcase and took a taxi here. Help me, Steve, I've nowhere to go, mate."

How could Steve react to those pleading eyes? They were beginning to fill up as Steve realised the plight he was in. Sean should have left home years ago and not stayed tied to his mother's apron strings so long. He had been a boy for too long. It was time to become a man. He felt secure with Steve around him and he badly needed security at that moment.

Steve knew this and played on it, reassuring him that everything would work out; that Sean's mother would come to see their willingness to live together. The only problem was could the pub support another mouth to feed and would Brian and Graham agree to Sean staying? That had to be tackled head-on. The first one to convince was Graham.

"Can we have a word, Gru," said Steve to his mate. "We need to discuss something concerning Sean."

"Ok, mate. Just let me finish cleaning up and I'll be right with you."

Graham had felt something was up when he saw Sean arrive and he knew his friend well enough to know that it was likely to be complicated. He went into the sitting room and saw an anxious couple greeting him.

"Who died, mate?" He joked.

"Nobody, but we have a problem and I'd like your advice on how to fix it."

"I'll try. What seems to be the problem?"

"Sean here has left home and wants to come and live with me. We're a bit of an item you might say. I've kept it quiet and haven't said much about it, but we've been seeing each other for a while now. But it looks like it's about to come out. You know me, I can't resist a pretty face, not for long anyhow. We obviously need to know how you feel about him living here. This is your business as well as mine, and he's got no money."

"I see." For a moment, Sean completely underestimated how far Graham would back his mate.

"Well, I mean when we get the kitchen going, we're going to need someone in the food department. Could you help us out there, Sean? Have you had any catering experience?"

"Yes, I've worked in cafés and restaurants in the summer when I was in college. I quite enjoyed it. I can't cook but I can wait on tables, help prepare food, serve in the bar. I promise I'll try to be as helpful as I can. I like Steve very much and would love to stay here!" He was beginning to sound a bit desperate and Graham didn't want to put too much pressure on him. He didn't want to do like a job interview.

"I can't see much of a problem here. You'll have to work and pull your weight, we can't carry anyone at the moment as we're not making enough for that. You'll have to work hard; the hours are long and there's a lot of cleaning to do in this old place. I think you'll cope though. But what about the sleeping arrangement? We've got four bedrooms but one's a joint room at the moment."

"He'll sleep in my room," said Steve. "I'll buy a mattress for him and he can bed down on that for a while."

"The only other problem in your father," said Graham. "How is he likely to take the news that you've left home?"

"Well, I left a letter for them before I came here. I explained that I was unhappy about living there and I wanted to move out. I just said I would be living with friends for a while. I didn't say anything about the pub."

"It won't take him long to work out where you've gone. He'll probably be around in the morning. Meanwhile, let's get your mattress sorted out. There's a spare one in the junk room," said Steve. "Help me to get it ready."

They were both were relieved that Graham was in agreement with the plan. Brian wouldn't be a problem and Angie would be grateful for another pair of hands in the kitchen.

It all depended on Sean's father. Sure enough, at eight o'clock the following morning, he showed up in the car.

Some of Sean's belongings were in a couple of suitcases he had brought with him. Steve went out to greet him.

"Morning, Mr Watkins, Nigel. Sean is here, he's safe and well. He arrived last night. Shall I call him for you? He's still in bed, he was exhausted last night."

"No, leave him, don't disturb him. Get him to ring me later. We read his note at night and his mother and I lost sleep worrying about what we should do. We feel that we've done as much as we can for the boy. We don't want to imprison the boy, he's a grown man. We guessed he'd be staying with you. We've packed his clothes, his CDs and sports gear. He's got a lot of stuff and much of it is still in his room. He's welcome to fetch the rest any time. Perhaps you'll also give him this."

He went to the back of the car and brought out an old teddy bear. He gave it to Steve.

"I know he is past the teddy bear age but it was his favourite and he used to keep it on his bed at home. Perhaps he'll settle a bit better if he has it."

"I'll make sure he gets it," said Steve, collecting the bags and suitcases.

"Do you want to come in for a drink?"

"No, thank you. It's a bit early for me. I'll get back to his mother. She's a bit upset, you see. You will look after my boy, won't you? Don't be rough with him, he's not much older than a school boy really. Tell him we still love him and will do anything we can for him."

Steve felt embarrassed and just stood there. "Well, I'll be off now. Tell Sean that if anything happens to let me know. Give him this for me." He took out his wallet and passed over a hundred pounds. Steve accepted it as he knew Sean would need it.

Mr Watkins got back inside the car and drove off, leaving Steve with all the belongings, wondering how it was all going to work out. Graham had a word of warning for his mate.

"You do know what you've doing, mate?" He asked. "This isn't going to be Cyprus all over again, is it?"

"What do you mean?"

"Letting your dick rule your brain. He's a nice boy, Sean, but he's young. What's to stop him running off with the first pretty rugby player he comes across? How secure is this relationship?"

"It's serious on my part. I think I'm in love with the boy. I feel relaxed in his company. I'm attracted to him sexually and I want to spend time with him. That for me is good enough. Don't worry, Graham. If it starts to go wrong, you'll be the first to know."

"That's good enough for me, mate. Let's see how we get on. I'll let Brian know about the new young tenant!"

"Thanks, Gra, I appreciate that."

Sean was in. They put an old mattress into Steve's room and he slept there, but more often than not, he and Steve ended up in Steve's single bed together in each other's arms.

Sean made sure he pulled his weight around the pub. He cleaned, polished and scrubbed as if the place was his. One thing that he made his own was the garden. Not much attention had been paid to the garden since they arrived, but it was the end of May now, and the garden was beginning to overgrow.

Nature was in danger of taking the place over. Martins had begun to make nests in the eaves of the roof. Collecting the mud from the nearby brook, they cemented the nest on securely and they could be seen coming and going busily all day. The tell-tale sign of white droppings could soon be seen under the nest announcing the arrival of chicks.

The grass was growing long at the back and the fruit trees had been in bloom for a few weeks now. It promised to be a bumper harvest. The lengthening days meant that more time could be devoted to keeping the grass trimmed and the bushes clipped. There were no more frosts after the middle of May so planting could begin. Brian had initially been pencilled in to keep the garden under control but it was too much for one.

Sean decided it was time he took control.

"I want to dig the garden over today," he announced at breakfast one morning.

"Ok," said Steve, not thinking it would be a big deal.

"I'd like to grow some vegetables and maybe use some of it in the pub and for our own use. What do you think?"

"I think you're on to a winning streak, young man," he said, hugging him affectionately and feeling his buttocks at the same time.

"Stop it, you are irritable. I can't keep you off," said Sean, grinning.

"I can't keep my hand off you," said Steve. "If it's too much, just knee me in the balls and tell me to grow up."

"Well, I can't see me doing that," said Sean, grabbing Steve around the middle and pulling him towards him.

"Come here, soldier boy, and kiss me," he ordered. Steve obeyed.

The garden was quite extensive, about an acre in size and leading to the brook at the end of it. The first job was to dig over the vegetable patch. There had been a vegetable patch there before but then Ken had abandoned it to weeds and bushes. Sean started with a spade and fork but it soon become obvious that this would take a long time to complete.

Steve decided to speed things up by getting a rotavator. He showed Sean how to use it and then let him get on with it. In a day, the whole patch was dug up. Sean put the weeds and unnecessary bushes in a heap and it formed the beginning of a compost heap of potatoes, tomatoes, peas, runner beans but overtime, he branched out into fruit tree and marrows. He even grew a beautiful row of sweet peas that attracted the bees in the full summer.

As the spring and early summer were so wet, the seeds took well and soon sprouted. Sean worked quietly and on his own for the whole afternoon in the warming sun.

The well-ordered lines of carrots and potatoes soon came into view. One good thing about gardening was that the fruit of your labour was soon visible. Runner beans started to grow up soon and wound their way to the top and the small, delicate summer promised a good crop. Because Ken hadn't grown anything for a few years, the soil didn't need much manure but Sean threw a few handfuls of bone meal over the fertile ground.

The crop of potatoes was pulled up in June. Sean loved to stay in the garden. It kept him out of the way of the others and he developed a healthy tan in the open air.

It was Sean that made the pub look attractive too. Hanging baskets appeared at the front of the pub; all lovingly watered during the warm summer night of June. Border plants like African marigolds and lobelia were planted along the side of the pub and off-set the stunning white of the newly painted walls.

The pub began to look pretty and Brian, in particular, noticed the difference.

"You're certainly making the place look attractive," he said one afternoon when they were both in the back on a slow shift.

"Thanks. I want to do my bit and show everyone that I care about the place."

"How's the garden coming along?"

"Ok, the runner beans are half way up the sticks and the rest of the potatoes need to be harvested soon. I have to thin out the carrots too. You could help me with that if you like."

"Sure, let's do it after tea."

"You don't mind me living here, Brian, do you? I know how hard you and the others worked to get this place up and running, and then I turned up like some Jonny come lately. Is that how you feel?"

"Not at all. You make Steve happy. He's a lot easier to be around than he was before. He could be a right grumpy sod at times but you stopped all that. No, mate, you're part of the team. Just don't let him down that's all."

"How would I do that?"

"By going with someone else; by abandoning all this for something more exciting perhaps."

"Believe me, this is as exciting as I want to get at the moment."

"It's the at-the-moment thing that worries me."

"Don't worry. I'm going nowhere. Where would I go to? London? I don't think it would suit me I'm a country boy at heart."

"Just don't be a cunt, that's all I'm saying."

After tea, the two boys busied themselves tidying up the vegetable patch. As they looked at the evening sun, they talked mostly about their respective fathers. Brian's had died recently and the memory was still fresh with him.

"He was a strange man, my father," he said as he dug into the soft earth. "My parents were in their mid-twenties when they married. My mother worked for him as a secretary and she sometimes cooked for him. He was an academic. He lectured in economics at the local Polytechnic. He wasn't the most organised of men.

"He was a bit of a mad professor, brilliant at his job but he wouldn't boil an egg. They met on a work trip together in Germany and when she got herself pregnant by him, they decided to marry. It was the seventies, post hippy time, peace and love and all that.

"They briefly fancied the hippy lifestyle. It was all incense and candles in our home. I can remember even now the smell in my bedroom when a candle was left burning too long. There were books everywhere. We had two dogs and it was a kind of organised chaos really. My mother told me never to interrupt my father when he was working and he worked hard at his job.

"I never looked for anything and he never hit me. I was given a fair amount of freedom and I appreciated that. That's how we were bought up then. They drank too much wine, and missed too many anniversaries. There were no pictures of them getting married. I presumed it was a rushed registry office job, my mother being pregnant and all.

"They could have been much worse parents but then they could have been better. They loved me but I think they were a bit disappointed that I hadn't done better at school. He wanted me to shine at something. I was good at a lot of things but not brilliant at one."

"I'm sure he loved you," said Sean. "I'm sure he was proud that you had a place at uni."

"That happened after he died. As far as he knows I'm a barman," he said sadly. Brian dug at a difficult root in the ground, he had to work it out with his spade.

"It's not that we disliked one another or anything, we just didn't seem to communicate much. When they discovered cancer just two years ago, I didn't know what to say to him. Mum told me about the illness, but he couldn't seem to tell me himself even in the hospital when I irritated him. I think he was embarrassed by it all. I tried to hold his hand once but he withdrew it quickly.

"He didn't want my sympathy. When I heard that he had died in the hospital, for a brief second, I felt glad. I felt released from him. Is that a terrible thing to feel?" He looked anxiously at the other boy who had his back to him.

"Not really. I think I understand. I don't have much in common with my father either. Maybe it's a generational thing. We speak a different language to him somehow. It shouldn't stop us from loving them though. Somethings are beyond words, don't you think?"

They dug up some potatoes and laid them in a pile even the small ones that clung to the net-like roots were taken and used. Brian dug up a row of carrots and then picked some strawberries for dessert the next day.

Sean rested on his spade and mused about his own father.

"My dad had planned out my whole life for me by the age of twelve. I wasn't a genius at school so he said better join him in the garage business. I went along with it for a while because I had nothing better to offer. I've never been a very ambitious person; perhaps that was my fault. It was never in my nature somehow to push myself forward.

"I can lazy, that I do recognise but it didn't take my dad long to realise that my heart wasn't in the business. Some boys must love living around in grease and oil, and getting their hands dirty, but it wasn't for me. I was a typical teenager. I fumed about with my hair, loved music and fashion, and eventually, going out and getting pissed, that seemed very normal to me.

"I know I was different from the other boys. I fancied the captain of the cricket team for ages. The amount of time I've wasted at cricket matches was all for nothing.

"He's married with a kid on the way now. Then you lot turned up and took over this place. I was delighted. New blood in the village and a hunk of an ex-soldier to drool over, what could be better? It was Christmas and my birthday all rolled into one. I'm really in a good place at the moment, Brian."

"Of course, you are, why wouldn't you be? Steve is a great bloke. I always got on well with both of them. But know where I stand with them if you mess up you get a bolloching that's fair. As I said though, don't let Steve down. He doesn't deserve that. He got thrown out of the army you know."

"No, I didn't know that," lied Sean. "Do you know why?"

"No, he didn't tell me but it must be serious. The army wouldn't have got rid of him for no reason. Perhaps he attacked someone; perhaps he killed someone. He's capable of it, he's a tough cookie."

"Maybe," said Sean. "I'll try to get it out of him. Come on, let's get this bloody garden sorted." He pretended to be engrossed in digging for a while but was actually thinking about what had happened in Cyprus on that night.

They decided as the sun dulled behind the trees to tackle the duck pond. Not for any reason being useful to the pub but because it would be beautiful and add beauty to the place. The curious mound of earth reflected in the bigger mound of earth surrounding the pub of local hills and copses had been calling out to be turned into a duck pond.

With spades and forks, they deepened the moat and flattened the top of the mound. Some kind of refuge for the ducks could be built on top, like a summer house in foxes or hounds were about. It took a couple of hours and they were both filthy at the end of it looking practical.

The moat ended up about eighteen inches deep and the mound could hold a refuge for half a dozen ducks, and he hoped Steve would pay for them. If not, he would save up. He thought the water from the kitchen could supply the moat and they could collect natural rain water to keep it topped up. Brian wanted gold fish in it but Sean wasn't so sure.

"I don't think they would survive," Sean said.

A twenty metre pipeline was needed to fill it up. When it was filled, it was a muddy pond with a curious mound in the middle but it would settle. Both boys seemed pleased with the result.

Sean had worked so hard with Brian to improve the look of the place that Steve thought he deserved a reward. He told him his ideas when they were lying in bed together that night.

"How do you fancy going abroad for a little break?"

"Really? Where to?"

"I was thinking Cyprus. You know I served there before I was discharged. I've always had a hankering to return and relive my army days."

"Are you sure that's a good idea? Won't it bring back some bad memories? You left under a cloud remember."

"That's partly why I want to go back to get those bad moments out of my memories of the place. You know it's a divided island, don't you? The Turks invaded it and took the northern part of the island leaving the Greeks with the rest. The best parts are in the north on the Turkish side. Our base was near the border but actually on the Greek side."

"It sounds interesting. I've never been to Cyprus before. Didn't Aphrodite originate from there? It sounds romantic."

"Yes, there are some wonderful beaches on the island. One, in particular, I want to show you."

"Is that the beach where you took that boy?"

"Yes, it is. Do you mind?"

"No, but I don't want to stress you out over all this. Maybe the past should be left in the past."

"I want to lay a few ghosts, that's all," said Steve, turning out the light.

"We've got ghosts enough, with the farmer's boy due to make an appearance soon," said Sean.

"Who said that?" Steve said in the dark.

They arranged with Graham to take a week off at the end of June. They would be staying at Ayia Napa, but first, they had to fly to Nicosia, the capital. They flew on British Airways. Graham drove the two and a half hour drive to Heathrow and wished them luck as he left them at Terminal 2. The flight only lasted three hours and the plane was due to take off at mid-day.

They decided to have a drink first at one of the bars in the terminal. Heathrow was relatively quiet. The schools hadn't broken up yet and it was the usual mix of business men, tourists and foreign tourists heading out east, or people going to the Middle East on contracts. They sat next to a lady who seemed to be crying. She looked at them nervously as they approached. She dried her eyes as the boys sat at her table.

"Do you mind?" Steve asked indicating the spare chairs.

"No, not at all, I'd be grateful for the company."

"Are you all right?" Sean asked, genuinely worried about her.

"Yes, I'm ok. I'm feeling homesick already and we haven't left the UK yet. Isn't that ridiculous?"

"Not at all. Where are you going?"

"Dubai. I've got a nursing job in one of the teaching hospitals, but this is my first time abroad. My family had a going away party for me at night in our local area, and to be honest, it just made it worse. All my relatives were there. My brother with his two kids, my mum and dad, my sister. I haven't stopped crying since. Where are you two going?"

"Cyprus, for a mini break. We're only going for a week but I'm excited as hell," said Sean.

"Great," said the nurse. "Treasure that feeling; don't let it get away. I could use feeling that way myself."

147

"Never mind," said Steve. "Try to enjoy it. Just think of all the good you'll be doing out there. I used to be in the army based in Cyprus and I always liked to think about the good things we would be doing for people. We helped out when the island was hit by an earthquake once. The people were so grateful, I'm sure you probably will feel the same."

"I hope so. I'm Ruth by the way." She held out her hand "I know this is ridiculous but when you get to your resort, will you send me a post-card? I'm known to make friends with people and have a great time. Tell me what the place is like and give me a glimpse of the night life."

The boys looked at one another, and Steve said, "I think we can go further and swap telephone numbers. Give us your number and we'll call you to make sure you arrive ok.

"You can tell us what Dubai is like. I've never been that way. Cyprus is the furthest in the south I've ever been. Is that a deal?"

Ruth was delighted. Suddenly, the whole trip had become a live trip rather than an ordeal, and he ordered another round of drinks.

"Cheers, fellas. I hope you both have a great time."

"Oh, I'm sure we will," said Sean, squeezing Steve's hand under the table.

"Are you looking for a girlfriend?" Ruth asked innocently.

"Not really," said Sean. "We're gay and we're together."

"Oh, I'm sorry but I never would have guessed. You both look straight."

"Thanks, I suppose that's a kind of compliment," said Steve who wasn't comfortable still about revealing his sexuality to strangers. Ruth, however, seemed nonjudgmental and accepting the boys' relationship as perfectly normal.

"It's great that you two are an item. I split up with my boyfriend last Christmas. That's partly the reason why I applied for a job abroad. I thought it might help me to get over my ex. I'm still not sure if I am over him yet. He's a fireman in Wood Green. I met him on the internet.

"I thought it was going great until I found out that he hadn't stopped seeing his ex-girlfriend. I found some e-mails that said he had met her and it was clear there was still something going on between them. I was so disappointed because I honestly thought he was the one. God, was he sexy in his uniform."

"I bet," said Sean.

"Steady, tiger, you know what you're like with uniforms and dressing up," said Steve.

"We split up when I confronted him with the evidence. He didn't attempt to hide it and said that he still loved Cath while he said that he loved me too. I know that he wasn't in love with me. Christmas was such a hard time for me. Why do these things have to happen at Christmas?"

"It's the whole wishing things to be other than they are," said Steve.

"People are dressing up, going to parties, drinking a bit too much and perhaps being a bit needy. Christmas is a time when people want something magical to happen to them, like Santa Claus. Life seems a bit unreal at Christmas. But don't let one bad experience put you off. Meet a nice, rich Arab who will take you away to his tent in the desert."

"Why, so that he can introduce you to his other three wives?" Ruth said, swinging off her glass of wine.

"Well, got to go, boys. They're calling my flight. Honestly, I hope you two. make it and have a lovely life together. Give me a ring in a couple of days, yeah?"

"Sure will and good luck," said Sean, kissing her on the cheek. They missed her when she was gone. Sean wanted to know more about her relationship and how it went wrong. What is it, he thought, about men and women that often one partner is not enough? Are we hard-wired to be promiscuous?

"I do feel a bit worried for her. She seems like a nice woman. I'm sure she would make a good wife for the right guy."

"That's the problem though, isn't it," said Steve. "Matching people with the right person. It's not easy, you can make more terrible mistakes."

"Do you think we are well matched?" Sean said, looking seriously at Steve.

"Of course, we are. Who could possibly put up with your insecurities if not for me? I love yer cos I fucks yer," he said in Herefordshire accent.

"Thanks, Steve, you really know how to make a girl feel really special," said Sean. "Is that our flight? Come on, let's go on holiday."

The flight was uneventful apart from some turbulence over the French Alps. Sean took hold of Steve's hand in mild panic.

"Don't worry, it's normal," he said and squeezed his hand gently. They could have been any two friends going over to a mate's stag night, thinking up strategies during the game and odd rituals designed to put the fear of God into the groom. But they weren't.

They were lovers looking forward to some time alone with each other so they could leave their past together. The rest of the world may as well not have existed as far as they were concerned. The only person in the world who mattered to them was sitting right next to them.

Neither man had been in love before so they were feeling their way along. It was a bit like trying to find the right way through a maze, both were determined to find the right way. They couldn't take things for granted though, not yet anyway. The flight attendants treated them with great care and attention, making sure they had everything they needed.

The gay male attendants guessed straightaway what the relationship was between them and were delighted in informing the girls what was really happening. The women loved it, even feeling a tad jealous.

They flirted with Steve to see Sean's reaction and it worked every time. Sean shot wild looks of jealousy as the women fussed around Steve, showing him the safety belts and how to make the rest go back. Both men were relieved when, after three hours or so, the captain announced that they were coming to land at the Nicosia airport.

"That was an eventful flight," said Sean, giving Steve a withering look.

"I'm surprised that blonde one didn't ask you for your phone number, she asked everything else!"

"Yeah, it's strange. In all the flights back and forth to England, I've never had that much attention before. What were they interested in? Surely, they could see we were an item. The way the blonde girl leant over us to pour the drinks was just embarrassing."

"Yes, it was. Girls do like a challenge though. Maybe they wanted to see if they could straighten us out a bit," said Sean.

"Not much chance of that though," he mused.

The boys were staying the first night at Nicosia in a three-star hotel. The hotel had an impressive man in a green suit greeting guests as they arrived. It had a pool and Sean wasted no time in going down to check it out…

It was thirty degrees in the shade and as he jumped in, he could feel all the stress of the last few months wash away from his body. He quickly swam a few lengths to get the frustration out and then he trod water in the deep end. Steve had gone to the kitchen, eager to find out what kind of food was on offer and if could they duplicate it at the Stag's Head. He appeared after half an hour and changed to join Sean in the pool.

"This is great," said Sean. "Why don't we just stay here for a week?"

"Because we're here to see the sea and a particular beach, remember?"

"This fucking beach better be good, that's all I'm saying, The amount of trouble it's caused," said Sean.

"The beach caused no trouble, I caused the trouble," said Steve. "It's where I lost my job and my reputation."

"Ok, I get it. What if you meet the same boy again, have you thought of that? It could be embarrassing."

"Mm, you're right as usual. I'll take the risk. I'd have to have really bad luck to bump into that cunt again."

"Of all the bars in the world, and you have to walk into mine," said Sean.

They frolicked in the pool for some time and it was obvious they were both becoming horny, so Steve suggested they retire to their room. Sean's heart began to beat wildly.

"Let me go up there first and prepare," he said exiting the pool and covering himself with a bath towel. When Steve got to the room, Sean was ready. He was naked on the bed, his penis erect.

Steve rounded the tables and pulled him to the side of the bed. Bringing his legs up, he fucked him from the front, making the boy gasp with pleasure. He was careful not to hurt him this time and they came quickly. He collapsed next to him and held him.

"Wow, you needed that," said Sean and kissed the top of Steve's head.

"Yeah, sorry. I couldn't hold that one back. Did I hurt you?"

"No, you were wonderful."

That night, they were tired and just went to the bar after dinner. It was intimate, with a married couple in the corner sipping cocktails. The two boys got two pints and sat down by the window. It was about nine and the sun was setting behind the body of buildings in the centre of Nicosia.

The couple stuck up a conversation.

"Thank God for that," said the man. "I was beginning to think we were the only ones who drank in this hotel."

"Quiet night," said Steve. "Maybe everyone else is out on the town."

"Or in their room trying to make sense of Greek TV. I'm Mark, by the way, and that is Suzie. We're from Manchester."

"Hiya. I'm Steve and this is my friend, Sean."

"Friend as in friend, or friend as in friend?" Suzie asked.

"The second one," said Sean as he held his hand out. "We've been going out together for a few months now."

"Good for you," said Mark. "We're pretty much open-minded about these things. Live and let live, I say."

"Glad to hear it," said Steve. "Are you two a couple? Married or anything. I don't see any rings."

"No, we're friends, good friends. I've been married but it didn't work out," said Mark. "I've known Suzie for a year now and we decided to holiday together to get away from it all, especially that Manchester rain. I run a small business supplying pubs and clubs around the Manchester area. Suzie is my secretary."

"What kind of things do you supply?" Sean said.

"Anything from rolls to beer coasters. We can even get you roller towels, soap dispensers and any kind of cleaning agent you can mention. We do a great line in rubber gloves. We can fit your pub or club out with all the silly items needed for a very competitive price. What's your line of business?"

"Strangely enough, we run a pub, a country pub near Hereford. We've been going for about six months now."

"Making any money at it? The pub trade isn't easy at the moment. This bloody recession is killing off a lot of good businesses. I could offer you a deal to cut your costs down to the minimum. Every penny saved is a penny on your profit."

"Hey you, I thought you said we weren't going to talk business. We're here for a break remember? The guys don't want to listen to your sales pitch," said Suzie, finishing her drink with a rattle of her bangles.

"Don't worry," said Steve. "We're here for the same reason but I like the idea of saving money. We can have a talk later maybe. Give me your number."

"Sure," said Mark, handing over his business card. It said Mark Holden, Supplier when it's Dire, pub and clubs. His telephone number had a Manchester code.

"Can we buy you a drink?" Sean asked, making his way to the small bar.

"Great. A vodka and lime for me and Mark's drinking lager."

"I was having a cocktail," he said.

"No, you have had enough of those," said Suzie. "It's time to go on a lager."

"Are you sure you are the boss?" Steve said smiling at Mark.

"He thinks he is," said Suzie. "But he couldn't organise a piss up in a brewery. I have to tell him to change his trousers sometimes. Well, customers notice that kind of thing."

"I'm not that bad," said Mark to Steve. He turned to Suzie. "And if you want a pay raise this year, learn some manners. I let her think she is in charge but she's not. She's the eye candy the punters see when they come through the door. I never argue with a woman, it's a waste of time."

"I'll drink to that," said Steve as Sean handed the drinks over. "Here's to a great holiday for all of us. Cheers, lads."

"Are you staying in Nicosia the whole time?" Mark asked.

"No, we're going by bus to Ayia Napa in the morning. It's about a two-hour drive."

"Make that three," said Mark. "The Greek roads are appalling. You'll have a great time in Ayia though. The place will be buzzing. I've done some business in those places, I know the clubs well there. They are noisy but generally good-natured. You won't find much trouble there. The Greek police won't stand for it."

"Oh, we can look after ourselves. I used to be in the army out here. I know what goes on here."

"Glad to hear. It has changed though; even in the last couple of years, I've noticed the difference. The punters are younger, drink more and are looking for wall-to-wall sex, of any description. The Greek Cypriots are pissed off having to deal with aggressive youngsters from Blighty. I can recommend some quieter places up the coast if you like, away from the strip."

"Yes," said Steve. "Give us more addresses. Any good restaurant you know of? I'm keen to try the cuisine. We want to offer food in the pub eventually. It would be good to offer some Greek dips, lamb goes down well where we are. The Greeks know how to cook lamb."

The couples were getting on well. The conversation was natural with no embarrassing pressure. Suzie didn't mind being the only woman present. She loved the company of men, didn't appreciate the competition from her own sex and always maintained she could get men to do whatever she wanted them to.

She was good-looking, wore a bit too much make-up and her long brown hair reminded Sean of the wig he wore for Ken that night when he dressed up for him. He looked at the bangles on her wrist, nine-carat gold mostly. She was smartly dressed but not overdressed. It didn't pay to flaunt one's wealth these days. She kept a small handbag close to her; she was probably carrying the money and Mark didn't seem to have a wallet on him.

He was dressed casually in chinos and a top. A sweater was around his shoulders but it wasn't needed on a warm night like this.

"Shall we take our drinks onto the terrace," suggested Mark. "It overlooks the pool."

They moved to the terrace and got a table by the pool which was empty. The moon was out and someone had switched on the lights around the pool. The crickets had started their singing but they only succeeded in adding to the atmosphere. Their constant chirping lulled then all to relax.

"You know," said Sean turning to Steve. "This is the first time I've felt as if I'm actually abroad. It feels different from Britain, more relaxing."

"That's the beer talking, young man," he said, "You're just getting bored."

"You're so romantic at times," he said. "Typical fucking squaddie."

"That's why you love me," he said and there was some truth in it.

Mark and Suzie retired early to bed, leaving the two boys alone by the pool. A slight breeze got up brushing their exposed skin in a deliciously warm way. The hair on the back of their arms came up and their senses seemed heightened somehow.

"This is nice," said Sean. "I am glad we came here. I feel relaxed with you."

"I know you do," said Steve stretching his legs before him. Both young men were relaxed and happy. Both were on the island of love and warmth; it didn't get much better than this.

"Shall we see if we can find a club?" Sean said.

"Not tonight," said Steve. "We have to catch the bus early tomorrow. If we got to a club, we'll probably get piss drunk and we'll be hung over in the morning. Let's leave it till we get to Ayia. I am enjoying it here anyway; you, the pool, the bloody grasshoppers."

"Ok," said Sean, "you're the boss."

"And don't you forget it, mister."

Chapter 10

They left Nicosia by bus early the next day. It was hot and sunny and the bus was crowded. They went to the back of the bus and that was a mistake. The Greeks grew their own tobacco. It's dark and strong, and they smoked it without filters, so after an hour or so, the atmosphere was smoky. Sean commented first.

"That tobacco is really strong; it's starting to turn my stomach. Do you think we could ask them to stop for a while? It seems like everyone on the bus is smoking except us. Haven't they heard of health and safety?"

"Probably not. You can open the window more, otherwise we could perhaps sit in the front. I'm sure they wouldn't mind."

"That's if he speaks English. I wouldn't like to bet on it," said Sean.

He watched the Cypriot scenery go by. When the island was divided in the seventies, the Turks took the best part of the island. They left a rocky, stony land, often littered and a bit depressing. Occasionally, they passed some orchards which contained lemons or oranges. Everywhere seemed parched. Only irrigation channels were keeping the fruit trees alive. The sky was impossibly blue with scattered clouds visible.

This part of the Mediterranean in summer resembled more like the Middle East than part of Europe. They went through small mountain villages where hardly a person was visible out in the hot sun. Tables of lotus fruit could be spotted outside certain homes and a stray chicken or two testified to some sort of life carried on here.

The occasional man spotted usually wore a dark suit with open neck shirt. The suit never seemed to fit properly. Many of the women wore black with a hand scarf to keep the sun off. The brown dogs lolled in the searing heat under trees if they were lucky, their mouths open to the dry air. No one moved very quickly.

After an hour and a half, the bus stopped at a road side cafe where the passengers could take some refreshments, use the toilet, or just relax in the air-conditioned booths. Sean and Steve bought some sandwiches and some bottled water. The choice was very limited.

"The quicker this lot joins the E.U. the better," said Steve picking up some feta cheese and a few black olives to go with the sandwiches.

"I agree, but you've been here before you were stationed here. You must have known it would be like this surely?" Sean said, tasting a black olive and immediately spitting it out.

"That's disgusting," he said, opening the water bottle to take a sip.

"You either love those things or hate them," said Steve. "Actually, once you're used to them, they're not that bad. Aye, aye, look at this guy." He indicated a short, stocky man wearing a singlet with a half apron who probably worked in the cafe. What caught the eye of both boys was the unmistakable bulge behind the apron.

"Fucking hell," said Sean, unable to contain himself. "Are you seeing what I'm seeing?"

"Can't miss it. I don't think it's a hard-on. I think he's just a big boy, which is unusual for such a short man. He's been well blessed anyway."

The boys took a table and watched. Sean was convinced he saw a cockroach crawl behind them as they pulled their chairs in. "I am not eating a meal here," he said. "The place is alive. Wait till we get to the hotel."

"Ok, let's just watch the floor show."

The driver of the bus had curled up in a corner and covered himself in a blanket to catch some sleep. The other passengers just got snacks and waited patiently for the driver to wake up. There was a queue for the only toilet. No one was in a hurry; no one complained about the amount of time the driver took to rest.

With the state of Cypriot roads being the way they were, it was best to have a driver who was well-rested and could bring his A-game to the increasingly hilly country. Sean couldn't take his eyes off the waiter and began to wonder what it would be like to have sex with him.

Perhaps his penis was one of those that didn't go up or down much, just stayed in a semi-erect state. Either way, he was dying to find out just what the small waiter had between his legs.

"Stop staring at the waiter," said Steve eventually. "You're making it obvious."

"Sorry," said Sean. "I don't mean to but I can't take my eyes off him. He's gorgeous."

"You'll see a few more men like him around here. The Greeks and the Turks for that matter are good-looking people. Your tongue is going to be hanging out for a week. Shall we see if we can get his phone number?"

"No, he might take offence, or shall we? We are on holiday after all. People do funny things away from home."

Steve beckoned to the waiter across and ordered two orange juices.

The waiter brought them promptly. He smiled as he put them on the table. That was enough for Steve.

"Greek or Turkish?" He asked.

"Greek, Sir," answered the man, waiting to be dismissed.

"We are going to Ayia Napa for a holiday. Do you know the town?"

"Oh yes, Sir, very nice town. Many boys and cafes; my brother works in one. I will write down the name of it. You will both like it. I think."

He went to fetch a pen and came back with a card on which he had written the name of the club along with his name and his brother's. The cafe was called Cafe Dionysus.

A telephone number came with the card.

"Ring us when you reach your hotel." His meaning was unmistakable.

"Your brother like you?" Steve asked, glancing at the man's bulge.

"Like me," said the guy. "Short but big."

Sean was squirming in his seat. "I can't believe you just did that," he said. "Are you going to ring him?" Sean asked playfully.

"I wouldn't mind taking a look, I must say. I just can't believe his dick is as big as it seems."

"Well, let's find out."

By now, the driver had woken up and had ordered everyone back onto the bus. The bills were paid and the journey resumed. Ayia Napa was another hour. They started the long torturous way towards the coast.

Little glimpses of the sea could occasionally be made out, although it was often difficult to distinguish the sea from the sky. The passengers on the bus were becoming excited as they rounded a bend, and there it was, the first expanse of the Mediterranean stretched out before them with Ayia Napa in the distance.

Ayia had started off as a pretty fishing village which advanced into a lovely resort catering more to the cheap end of the market. 'Thalassa, thalassa', they heard as they crept towards it. Hotels and bars started to appear, open already to the early punters, those who hadn't drunk themselves stupid the previous night. The traffic increased and young people dressed in t-shirts and shorts mostly criss-crossed the harbour area enjoying the sun.

"Looks like the action has already started," said Sean, trying to take it all in and feeling excited. There were English signs everywhere—'Full English, English spoken here, English welcome, John bull, cheque open twenty-four hours'. Communication was not going to be a problem.

"Let's get to the hotel first and unpack," said Steve. He had been here before and had mixed feelings about being here again. This time, he was determined to stay in control and to limit his drinking. He wanted to have a good time but he also had business to see to. He had a past to confront.

They arrived at the hotel by taxi. It was a short journey from where they had been dropped off by the bus station. The hotel wasn't as good as the one in Nicosia. It was a non-descript square building on a side street of Ayia.

It was about a ten-minute walk from the harbour. Attempts had been made to soften the harshness of the concrete by positioning large terracotta pots containing ferns and grasses around the entrance. The boys went straight to reception and signed in. The receptionist wanted to keep their passports.

"Don't worry, Sir, they will be kept safe," he said mechanically.

"But why do you need to keep them?" Steve asked, a bit annoyed.

"This is all-inclusive holiday, we've paid the bill already. Yes, but maybe you will incur other charges while you are here at the bar or restaurant for example. We have had customers refuse to pay in the past. If you don't have your passports, you cannot decide suddenly to leave the country without paying that's all."

"I see," said Steve. "Okay, but I'm not happy about it. I've never had to give up my passport before in Cyprus."

"When we join the E.E.C, it will become obligatory, I can assure you. Here are your keys."

He handed the keys over and the boys got in the lift to the first floor. The room was smaller than in the hotel in Nicosia. And there was no pool in the hotel. They would have to use the sea.

"What's wrong with you?" Sean asked, looking at his friend closely. "You seem edgy and angry. I haven't seen you like this before. Ever since we arrived at this town, you've gotten jumpy."

"Sorry, I know this, it's like visiting the scene of a crime. Maybe it was a mistake to come here. There are other fishing villages along the coast just as pretty. Perhaps we should have gone to one of them."

"Relax, buddy, you've got me here to protect you. I won't let anything bad happen to you here. If it all gets too much for you, we will move on somewhere else. We're on holiday, remember."

"Thanks, Sean, you're a star. Makes a change for you to be looking after me. I want to give you the holiday of a lifetime, that's all."

"Stop trying so hard and relax. Come on, take a shower and let's eat."

They had lamb cutlets and salad for lunch, and washed it down with a bottle of wine, and life suddenly seemed a lot easier. They rested in the afternoon and then got ready to go out in the evening. It was hot, a light breeze blowing in from the Mediterranean. Both men wore shorts and singlets. Sean again carried the money.

"Where shall we go tonight?" He asked casually, secretly knowing what the answer would be.

"You know where I want to go," said Steve. "The bar where I met that lad. It's called the Rodeo. There are some real cowboys there, believe me. Once I have seen the place and had a good drink there with you, I can relax and enjoy myself. Okay, but any sign of stress and I am getting you out of there."

"Agreed."

They walked casually through the narrow streets of the harbour town. They were just two more young men in a sea of young men. Some in big groups, others into twos and threes. They looked around the shops but they weren't there for souvenirs. The atmosphere was exciting and noisy.

They recognised different accents of the UK everywhere they went. Young lads and girls all wanting a good time and a few laughs. As they approached the spot where most of the bars and heavy drinking took place, the atmosphere changed. It became louder and more raucous. The air became filled with obscenity and more threatening language.

Sean was looking a bit more nervous and stayed close to his man. Steve began to spit on the street and unconsciously opened and closed his fists.

"There are lads from Manchester and Liverpool here. I can recognise the accent; keep your eyes sharp. The bar is just twenty yards further on."

The Rodeo was just like all the other bars on the strip but bigger. Music blared from a sound system and the bar was busy with youngsters. Drinking games were in progress and with laughter and guffaws breaking out now and then. There was a large mechanical bull in the centre of the pub surrounded by a crowd.

If you could ride the bull for more than thirty seconds, you get free drinks for you and your mates. Many guys gave it a try and few succeeded.

A group of lads got up and left to go somewhere else. Steve grabbed the table.

"That's handy. What do you want to drink?"

"I'll start with a lager."

"Don't move and don't let anyone take the seats." He went to the bar and was gone for some time because the place was getting busy. It was a pity that the Stag's Head wasn't like this most nights, otherwise they all would be millionaires. Sean studied the crowd around him.

Most were in their early twenties, British, and most were drunk. A lot of tattoos were visible either to get the attention of the girls or war scars to show other boys. It was only eight o'clock but the party was in full swing.

A young lad of nineteen or twenty came up towards one of the empty chairs. He was handsome, strong and tall, with both arms full of tattoos. His muscles flexed as he grabbed the back of the chair. "Can I?" He said.

"Go ahead," said Sean, unable to deny him anything.

They were down to three chairs. Steve came back with a couple of drinks and sat so that he could survey the whole bar. He had already worked out exit strategies in the event of trouble breaking out. He had identified possible trouble makers at the bar and worked out where the security was situated if he needed them.

It wasn't so much a night out as a plan of action with worst-case scenario in mind. It was his army training that he was using, aided by his natural instinct which most sexually active males learned to develop. He needed to protect his mate if they were attacked and he needed to warn him of any danger.

"Just keep an eye on that big bastard with no top standing at the bar. He could be trouble. I heard him run his mouth off against gays when I was at the bar. He could be a nasty piece of work."

"Yes, I did notice him. He's quite pissed and he's got a few mates with him," said Sean, eyeing the boy carefully.

The atmosphere lightened considerably when a party of women showed up, all dressed as nuns. The boys gathered round making loud comments and offering to buy the drinks.

Steve relaxed visibly when the group of boys he was most worried about moved on to another bar.

"Johnny, Luke, come on. Let's move on. There are too many proofs here." Steve could see that the comment wasn't aimed at them, but a boy drinking with a friend at the far end of the bar. Steve observed them closely.

"I don't believe it," he said under his breath. Sean could make out where he was looking.

"Do you know them?" He asked.

"I think it's him; think it's the boy I went with that night. He's changed his appearance. I don't remember the short-cropped hair but it's him all right. I don't know his friend."

The two guys were just standing and drinking like everyone else, but the boy looked around and saw Steve eyeing him. He seemed to recognise Steve and said a few words to his friend. They both come across.

"Hello, soldier boy, we meet again. Do you remember me?"

"How could I forget you, you cost me my job."

"Oh, yes. That was a shame and a surprise. I hoped that they would fine you, not send you back to England. I am sorry for that."

"How are you anyway, Andre? Who's your friend?"

"I don't know his name, I just met him. He seems very nice. He's German, I think, or Austrian. You seemed very nice when I met you. A saying in English: don't judge a book by its cover."

"Would you like to sit down and have a drink with us?"

"There are only three seats," said Andre. His friend stood.

"I see you have found yourself another pretty boy accompanying you. Introduce me to him," said Andre.

"This is Sean. We've been friends for a few months now."
Sean nodded but kept quiet. There was something about the
Greek boy that unnerved him. A tendency to be over-familiar
perhaps. Sean noticed the tiredness behind the eyes, boredom
even and the sweat on his forehead. Andre didn't look well.

"So how have you been keeping?" Steve asked genuinely
concerned for him.

"Not so good. After you left, the army gave a warning to
the other soldiers to stay away from the bars at night. They
were scared of being sent home like you, so they don't come
to the strip much these days. It's hard for boys like me to make
a living now. Sometimes the German boys are generous but
not often.

"They come and go as they hate the drinking games and
the fighting, so they go further along the coast to quiet spots.
I love it here though, the music and the crowd. Hardly anyone
goes to our special beach anymore. Such a pity cause it's
really quite beautiful, especially at night.

"It's so remote and it has been tough since you left. God
help me, I may have to take a bar job to survive, that's how
bad it is."

"I'm sorry to hear that, Andre," said Steve. "You're
getting too old for this now, Andre. How old are you
actually?"

"I am twenty-two now. I was a young boy when you had
me that night. You hurt me that night that's why I complained
about you and you refused to pay me, but I must admit, you're
hot as hell and you know what you are doing. You were the
best I ever did it with you know that?"

Andre turned to Sean and asked him, "Has he hurt you yet when he fucks you? Or can you handle him?" He looked at Sean boldly.

"Wow, what a question! But since you ask, yes, he hurt me once but we've discussed all that and now there's no problem. He is just a bit energetic that's all. You understand that word?"

"Yes, I understand but it's more than energetic. He wants to control and punish for something else, something different, darker."

"I don't allow him to control me," said Sean spiritedly. "I control him."

"He is a soldier, don't forget, he's trained to kill. But he's also trained to take orders, he has to from the officers, yes, but when they are on their own, they like to control. They're trained how to kill I agree with you, but what if they go too far? What happened then? They know how to survive in difficult situations. Once you have trained a strong man to do that, you have created a monster."

"Andre's eyes were shining at this point," and his sweating increased.

"Is that how you see me, Andre? A monster?"

"No, you are a pretty boy who has been trained to be a killer. This is a pretty boy. What do you do now?"

"We own a pub in England called the Stag's Head. It's an old country pub in the middle of nowhere. You must come to England and visit us. You can stay as long as you like."

"I may do that sometime. I haven't felt well lately so maybe it is time to take a break from all of this." He indicated the whole bar which was full now and becoming louder.

"Get yourself a boyfriend," said Sean. "Someone who will look after you and care for you. You are a good-looking boy, you must have admirers."

"Old men mostly. They don't turn me on but they pay the rent. I did meet one very nice American guy last year. He was about forty. He was actually here with his wife but she didn't know about his secret or so he thought. How we kept it from her I don't know.

"Women are like gays, they have a sixth sense. They can tell if their husbands are cheating on them. Then what do you know? I see her on the harbour's wall one day with some short Greek guy making out. She was cheating on her husband."

"Could be the brother of our friend in the cafe," said Steve to Sean.

"Sounds like it. This is a small town after all. She knew about her husband and just wanted to turn the tables."

"Shall we move on? This place is giving me a headache," said Steve.

The bar was full now and becoming riotous. It was time to move on.

"Take care, Andre. I'm glad we had a little chat. I mean it about visiting us in England. You must come and stay when all this gets too much."

"Thank you both of you. Sorry about you losing your job but it looks like things have worked out well for you. If you hadn't left the army, you couldn't have met this guy," he said, indicating Sean.

"True, true," said Steve.

Andre turned to his friend and they both drank and melted into the melee that was the night time crowd.

"Do you believe all that nonsense?" Sean said.

"What about me being a monster?"

"And about the control and domination."

"I can be a bit of a control freak, I'll admit that, but I don't get jealous. If you wanted to go off and have sex with another man, I am not going to stop you. You have your needs, I have mine. I'd hope to be enough for you but who knows. You're taught how to kill in the army but it's controlled aggression, a bit like a boxer. I can switch it on and off."

"He doesn't seem so bad," said Sean referring to Andre.

"He's changed," said Steve. "He's grown up beautifully, though he used to be a lot wilder than that, especially with a few drinks in him. He needs to find someone special soon though. He didn't actually look very well. Come on, let's go. There is one more place I want to show you tonight."

Chapter 11
The Bay

The boys left the noise and chaos of the bar and went out into the warm night. There was a full moon that night and the sky was clear and speckled with stars. This was a night for love. They walked along the harbour and out along the shore.

Steve knew where he was going, he had made that trip before. He had his arm around the boy's neck and occasionally kissed him on the side of his head.

Sean had his arm around Steve's waist and would now and then brush his fingers along his buttocks. It felt like an electric charge going through his body.

The bay was a good mile down the coast and it took them half an hour to reach it. Sean could understand why it was popular with couples because although the beach was small, it was hemmed in by rocks of different sizes. Behind some of them were small areas where you were unseen from the main part.

You could relax here confidently as you wouldn't be observed by any late walkers. They were the only two on the beach. Steve led the boy to the exact same spot where he had taken Andre that night. They say you should never go back it's always a mistake; Steve was out to prove that saying wrong tonight.

They sat on the sand and watched the stars. The moon detracted from the Milky Way but enough could be seen to reveal a spectacular backdrop to their love making. It was like an old theatre lit by candles and prepared for the major performance.

The candles cast shadows that danced in the slight breeze and ghostly shapes waved from every side. The very rocks were spectators to the act the rippling sea, an excited murmur of an expected audience.

"Whatever happens tonight," said Steve. "I promise you I won't hurt you."

"I believe you, big squaddie; come here."

Sean initiated the lovemaking. He wanted him so badly he couldn't wait for the older man. They both quickly stripped and lay naked on the sand. It felt strange to the touch and the sand stuck to the skin. Steve kissed the boy all over, nuzzling him on the inside of his legs and on his cock and balls.

Sean shivered as the balls hardened under the touch. His cock was impossibly hard by now. Steve straddled the boy, putting his cock against his mouth. The boy responded and sucked him greedily. They both began to moan and rock in rhythm. Within minutes, Steve was ready but the sand was a nuisance, it got into every orifice possible.

"There's sand everywhere," said Sean. "What can we do?"

"Come to the water, I'll take you there." He pitched the lad up and carried him to the water's edge, allowing the ripples of the waves to wash him clean of the sand. The reflection of the moon glistened on the boys' skin making it

174

look oily and lubricated. The light danced on the waves around them and both men were covered slightly in salty water. The push of the waves encouraged Steve to begin his action, and turning the boy, he put his penis against the boy's buttocks. Sean yielded and raised his thighs up above the water and felt the urgent cock push in. The water washed them with each thrust, and Steve contented himself without pushing the whole cock in.

He seemed to move in rhythm with the sea and each wave made Sean gasp. Steve was ready to ejaculate; giving the boy three or four strong thrusts, he could feel the liquid travel up to the head. The man pulled out and shot the milky substance into the sea like some fish fertilising the eggs of the female by hit or miss.

The pearly globules sank to the sea floor and disappeared in the brine. They mingled with the rocks and sand, and eventually dissolved. Steve collapsed on top of him, spent and satisfied.

Neither of them moved for some time, content to let the waves wash them, but eventually, Steve picked the boy up and took him further up the beach.

"Are you ok?" He asked.

"Yes, thank you. Let's just relax for a bit."

They lay on their backs and followed the rotation of the earth as the stars wheeled above them. Sean trailed his fingers through Steve's hair. Sean broke the spell.

"Why does nobody call you Steven?" He asked innocently enough. "Can I call you Steven?"

"If you like. It's better than squaddie or soldier boy. Only my mother ever called me Steven and really when she was angry with me. I used to wind her up a bit. Then she would

175

tell me off if I got too cheeky. She was a good mother though, a wonderful cook, and she allowed me and my sister a lot of freedom."

"You've got a sister. I didn't know that. I really don't know you at all, do I? Do you have any brothers?"

"No, just the one younger sister. We used to fight like cats and dogs. She is married to a copper; they live in Evesham. I visit them occasionally."

"Anything else I should know about you?"

"Only that I fancy the fuck out of you. I love your honesty and openness. I love the way you trust me, that's rare in two guys. I can't get enough of your arse; it makes me horny as hell."

"Glad to hear it. I think it's my best feature. And what about Andre now? Have you got him out of your system or is he always going to be in the background as a feeling of regret?"

"I'll never forgive myself. I brought him here for sex and sex only. I was drunk, he was tipsy and used him like an animal. I am not proud of that, actually feel ashamed of it. Then not paying him as well as giving him a thick lip was another insult. I can understand why he did what he did.

"I deserve it. I've paid the price for that night, but since it meant meeting you, I feel like it's not all bad. You have turned me from a spoiled boy into a real man, and I am grateful for that."

"So, what shall we do now? I am actually starting to feel cold. Shall we get dressed again? It's not too late. We could have a night cap before going back to the hotel," said Sean.

"Yes, but not the Rodeo. I'd prefer somewhere quieter where we can chat and look at the stars," said Steve.

"Agreed."

They found a bar that looked over the harbour and they sat outside and watched the boats prepare for another night of fishing. As the last boat left the harbour, they got up and arm in arm, walked slowly back to the hotel.

Chapter 12

The next few days were spent mostly on the beach. Steve spoiled the lad buying him presents from the local gift shops. He bought him new sunglasses and a baseball cap that made Sean look like a drug dealer. Sean told him that he didn't need to buy his love but it made Steve feel good.

One day, he bought him an expensive silver bracelet with 'SS' engraved. Sean never removed it, not even in the shower. He looked up to the older man interested in him implicitly. It was a mixture of love and worship.

One day, Steve was tired and had a slight cold. Sean took care of him, making him drinks and saying they shouldn't go down to the beach that day.

When he regained his strength, he was delighted with him and kissed him. They religiously went down to breakfast each morning and had an omelette or just toast and coffee. The hotel staff accepted them without hesitation. It didn't seem odd to them to have two fit men sharing a room together. The cleaner maid caught them kissing in the corridor once, but she just smiled at having her suspicions proved true.

Towards the end of their stay, Steve's mobile rang. It was the waiter from the café. He was in town and wanted to meet them.

"Sure," said Steve. "Meet us in the Mt Athos café at twelve."

They were both pleased to see him. His name was Lukas and he was having a break for a few days. He intended to look up his brother who worked in the town. He carried a red hold all with an image of the Parthenon on it.

"How are you two enjoying yourself? The weather is good, not too hot and the hotel is looking after you?" He enquired.

"The weather is perfect, it's a party. There is no pool but apart from that, it's fine," said Sean, giving him a smile.

"Where are you staying?" Steve asked.

"With a friend. You say mate in English, I think."

"Yes, if he is a good friend," said Sean.

"Are you two mates?" Lukas asked with a smile.

"More than mates now," said Steve clasping Sean's hand.

"That's nice. It's good to see two good-looking men getting on so well. I am a bit jealous," said Lukas.

"You don't have a boyfriend?" Sean asked.

"No, things are not so easy here. You have to pretend to like women, otherwise it can cause problems for you and your family. These are small towns and people get annoyed quickly, you understand?"

"We understand. You will find someone too I am sure, if not from here, then a foreigner. You can always go to a hotel together."

"Sometimes, although the beach is probably safer. I'd love to see your hotel and spend some time with you both. It's not so easy with another Greek. There is a lot of honour involved, if you understand me."

He looked lonely as if he badly needed company. Sean and Steve looked at each other and were unsure about what to do but they liked Lukas and trusted him.

"One thing we noticed when we were in your cafe was the size of your penis. You seem like a big man; is it true?" Steve said genuinely curious.

"You want to have a look?" Lukas asked playfully.

"Oh, yes. A good look," said Sean, blushing slightly.

"We are a quiet and open-minded couple and we like the idea of experimenting, but only with the right person. We're on holiday so what the hell. You could come back to our hotel and have a drink there."

"Sure, I've brought my box of tricks with me as well," he said, indicating the hold-all.

The two lads couldn't resist a challenge and wanted to see what was in the bag, but Lukas wouldn't open it not in public. They all walked back to the hotel feeling slightly nervous about what was to happen, but they would have felt frustrated if they had said no. To calm the nerves, they took a drink in the bar and then went up to the room.

Lukas disappeared in the bathroom. The boys closed the blinds, locked all the doors and waited. He took a long time but when he appeared, it was worth waiting for. He was completely naked with a huge erection, hard and strong. He had covered it with a large black condom.

It took their breath away. Both were looking at him in admiration. He looked like the Greek God, Priapus, the god of sex with a huge member.

"Fucking hell, you are a boy. I've seen some big lads in the army but nothing like this," said Steve.

Lukas looked down a bit sheepishly and took the cock in his hand.

"It's a real handful," he said. He gave it to Sean who handled it.

"I've brought some toys for us to play with," he said, indicating the bag.

Steve opened and inside lay a sort of sex toys of various sizes. There were nipple clamps, butt plugs, and dildos of varying thickness and length. He counted and there were eight thick, black, flexible dildos to play with.

"Who's first?" He joked.

"This is out of proportion to your body," said Sean, still playing with Lukas' cock. "Isn't it a problem for you?"

"It can be. That's why we need this," and he pulled out two large bottles of baby oil from the bag. He also pulled out a six-foot-long piece of strong silk, like a tie.

"What that for?" Steve asked, thinking of bondage.

"I'll show you," said Lukas.

The other two lads stripped off and Lukas took control. He was very experienced in love making. A series of one-night stands in his hometown had taught him some tricks. They put towels from the bathroom on to a study table that was in the room. They got Sean onto the table, his legs dangling over one side and his head on the other.

They stood over him one on each side. They were like two priests about to sacrifice some poor animal but it had to be done the right way. Lukas got the oil and covered Sean with it. His body glistened and shivered slightly to the touch. Lukas had strong, horny hands and they felt rough to Sean. He loved the feel of the oil though. It got everywhere.

Steve played with Sean's cock and got it hard. The head throbbed in anticipation. Lukas got the long tie and tied the middle of it around Sean's cock and balls. Then each end was bound around his ankle so that he was trussed up like a turkey. If he moved too much, it pulled on his balls. He was helpless.

Steve was fascinated. He hadn't seen that one before. Pushing the boy's leg a bit higher, his buttocks were completely exposed. Steve covered him in more oil around his orifice. Sean moved in delight and cooperated fully in the game. His head dropped down the other side of the table and Lukas introduced his member to Sean's mouth.

Sean sucked him hard but the rubber of the condom was annoying.

Steve was ready to penetrate at the other end.

He rubbed his cock playfully against the orifice. He got about an inch in, and with so much lubrication, it went in easily. Sean moaned; he was being played at both ends and he just gave into it; he wanted to please both older men. Steve pumped slowly and got deeper. He didn't want to hurt the boy so he moved carefully.

They both pumped the boy until he had enough; it was getting uncomfortable now. It needed to stop. Lukas was ready and pulled out, spouting into the condom. He felt exhausted. Steve wasn't ready though; maybe the presence of the other man was putting him off.

"Shoot for fuck's sake, I can't take anymore."

"I am not ready unless you play the game we said we wouldn't play anymore. I have to get aggressive with you, then I will come."

"Ok, do it, do it."

"I'm going to punish you, boy. You've been a naughty boy again, haven't you, haven't you?" Steve demanded.

"Yes, punish me, Steve. Yes, just fucking punish me." As Steve became more aggressive, Sean's moans became more like a whisper as he dominated deeper. Sean felt the cock throb and got harder as the fluid shot deep in him.

Steve lay on his boy's buttocks still inside him. He withdrew gradually and collapsed on the bed with Lukas beside him. Nobody said anything for some time, and then they untied Sean and let him rest.

"Well, here we are again then," said the boy bitterly.

"Sorry. What can I say, we got carried away again. This is so intense."

"Yes, but I am the one with the sore arse. Why do I find big men so attractive? I am having a shower."

Lukas was abashed. He had disposed of the condom but still lay naked on the bed. His erection had hardly altered.

"Is your friend okay, Steve?" He asked, concerned.

"Yes, although, I promised him I wouldn't get like that again. I've broken my promise. He'll be ok, just give him a few minutes on his own."

"Do you want me to go?" Lukas asked.

"No," said Steve. "Stay and have something to eat with us. I'll order something from the kitchen, they'll leave it outside the door. We need to talk, all three of us."

The order came soon after and they ate together in silence for a while. Steve got three small bottles of wine from the fridge.

"Where are you going now, Lukas?" Sean asked.

"I'll stay with my brother, Dino, for a while. He has a small flat above the cafe where he works. I thought of writing him to meet you two but he doesn't speak much English and it's very busy in the cafe now. Maybe I can introduce him to you some other time."

"Is he like you?" Sean asked.

"Yes, he's a big man; he's taller too. Did you enjoy what we did for you? We wanted to please you."

"I know you did but now I know what the expression means, you can have too much of a good thing."

"Did it turn you on?"

"Of course, it did," said Sean. "That's what I'm worried about. I like the humiliation too much. I love feeling used and abused. What does that say about me?"

"That you're up for a good time," said Steve, weakly. "gay sex could be a problem for me. I enjoy it too much and let all my inhibitions go out the window."

"Don't forget, you're abroad. People do crazy things when they're away from home. You had two guys making love to you because they both like you and because one of them loves you very much."

"Loves me or just loves my arse," he replied.

"Loves every bit of you. Let's just lie together and relax."

The three men lay on the bed together naked, little Sean in the middle, and dozed for an hour in the afternoon. Sean awoke to find Lukas rubbing against him yet again.

It was always difficult to tell with Lukas if he had an erection or not. His dick didn't seem to go down much after sex and was in a constant state of ready. Sean pulled him away and got up to have a drink, leaving the older men together.

He sat in a chair and watched them. It was obvious that Lukas was ready to go again and he tried his luck with Steve.

Steve was facing away from him and he felt Lukas move against him. He didn't try to resist him. Lukas put his cock between Steve's legs and found him receptive. He needed no other invitation. To Sean's delight, Lukas gave Steve a taste of his own medicine. Putting his arm around him, he got him in a vice-like grip that was difficult to get out of.

He mounted the other man and coupled with him using the leverage of his arms to penetrate deep. Steve could only lie there and take it. Lukas took some time to come and when they were finished, both men were bathed in sweat.

"That's what I call fucking a big dick," said Lukas.

Sean found he had masturbated himself watching the two men fucking. It was too much. All three men were exhausted now and they quickly showered and got dressed.

Lukas kissed both of them, called a taxi and left to go to his brother's. Steve and Sean were alone together again.

"Maybe we should talk about how to deal with it," said Steve.

"Deal with what?" Sean asked.

"The sex, the pressure, the desire," he said.

"We can deal with it but maybe just two of us. Perhaps getting Lukas over here was a mistake."

"Yes. Magnificent though he is," said Steve.

"Oh, he's magnificent all right. Such a cock of that size on a guy who's only five-four or five-five."

"A freak of nature," said Steve. "Although, it works the other way round. Impressive big guys can have small cocks, isn't nature wonderful?"

"Well, you're quite enough for me. There's no real damage done and the holiday is coming to an end. Perhaps it's time to get back to normality and start work again."

"Yes, Graham rang. Everything is okay at the pub. There's been a coroner's inquest about Ken apparently. They said it was suicide as the balance of his mind was disturbed."

"I am beginning to know how he felt," said Sean. "All this sex is disturbing my balance too. For the last day, let's visit somewhere interesting. Bar and clubs are business holidays for us. You could ask the address if there are any places worth visiting that are local."

"Good idea," said Steve, bored with bars and shopping.

Maria was at reception when they went down the following morning.

"Kalu Mere," she intoned smiling at them. She secretly held the hots for Steve even though she was married with three children.

Maria said, "Steve, good morning."

"It's our last full day and we don't want to waste it. Are there any sites around Ayia worth seeing? We don't want to spend our final day here in a bar."

"You could visit the church where St Paul preached around 60 AD. It's about five miles from here. You will need a taxi."

"You mean the St Paul conversion on the road to Damascus St Paul. I didn't realise he came to Cyprus."

"Oh yes, he preached in a beautiful little church near here on his way to the mainland. He was born in Antioch you know."

"No, I didn't know. I must admit I don't know much about St Paul. Hasn't he got a reputation for being a strict kind of Christian?" Steve said.

"Yes, I think that's why we Greeks love him so much. Shall I call for a taxi?"

"What do you think?" Steve asked.

"I think we could go and have a look. We should do something cultural while we're here," said Sean.

"Okay, ring for a taxi, Maria, please."

The taxi was there in no time. It was her brother's business. Maria quickly explained where to go; the driver knew it well.

"You'll love the church. It's for all the Saints but especially St Paul. We Greeks are strange people when it comes to religion," he said. "You know that if a boy or girl dies before they got married, we bury them in the marriage clothes."

"Why?" Sean asked, fascinated.

"Because marriage is the most important part of life and if the person has not had the chance to marry when they were alive, at least they can look married when they are dead."

"That seems strange to me," said Sean. "But we also dress people up before putting them in the coffin. It's the final respect we can pay them."

"We like to remember the dead," said the driver. "If you go to a Greek cemetery at night, you'll find the place lit up with candles and pictures of the dead person on the grave so we don't forget them. They find it hard to say goodbye to them."

"We are going to be in a Greek cemetery if you drive like this," said Steve. "Keep your eyes on the road, man."

"Sorry," said the driver, concentrating at last.

They drove out of Ayia up into the hills surrounding the town. They found themselves in a little town called Liopetri. It had a small square in the middle where the church of all the Saints was situated. They got out at the small, squat church, which had a notice on the front door that said, 'St Paul preached here'.

They arranged for the taxi to pick them up three hours later. If the church wasn't very interesting, at least they could have a look around the town and maybe go for a meal somewhere. You didn't have to go far to find a Greek restaurant.

Not many people were wandering around the town but that was because so many were in the church. There were a christening going on in the church. Going from the bright light into the gloomy candle light interior took some getting used to.

They could make out statues of Jesus on the cross and Mary holding baby Jesus near the front. What struck the boys was the amount of activity going on amongst the congregation. In Britain, the congregation tend to stay in their place except for mass. Here there were children playing in the aisles and talking to their friends.

People came and went crossing themselves after; little attention was being paid to what was happening at the religious end. Two children were being confirmed into the Greek orthodox church. One was a boy of about seven; the other was a handicapped girl in a wheelchair. The girl was older, perhaps twelve. The boy was carried in the large white towel.

In front of the priest, who were also in white, was a large pot half filled with water. It looked like an enormous cooking pot. Electric fires were burning everywhere. Some positioned around the pot. The two lads were in two minds about whether to stay but something held them there. They took a seat near the back.

The priest had a huge black bible open in front of him and he was reading from the text. He started to stumble over the words occasionally. He was a young priest and he had to repeat certain words. The boy in the towel was called from his seat and made to stand by the pot.

At a given signal, he untied the white robe and took it off. He was completely naked underneath. The two lads at the back were amazed and wondered what was going to happen next. The boy was quite tall even for a seven year old. So two young priests came up, caught him under his arms, and lifted him into the pot.

Now it was clear why there were so many electric fires everywhere; it was to keep the young lad warm when he was exposed. The priest approached and continue to mumble all the time, and he ducked the boy's head under the water three times.

The boy was then hauled out of the pot and anointed with holy oil in the shape of the Cross all over his body, his forehead, his cheek, his chin, his arms and shoulders, his legs and feet. The sign of the Cross was put all over him.

Steve turned to an old lady sitting next to him and asked what was going on.

"He's a refugee from Albania," she said. "The Communists didn't allow any religion there but when the regime collapsed, they allowed Greeks to cross the border. Some have come to Cyprus if they have relatives, and one of the first thing they must do is to christen the children."

"And the oil?" Sean asked. "What is the point in making the sign of the Cross all over his body?"

"To stop the devil getting in," was the reply. "It's an old tradition to cover him everywhere in the Christ's cross, of course, they should have been done when they were babies. The boy did very well, didn't he? He didn't panic or struggle. His parents must have explained carefully to him what he had to do."

"And the girl?" Sean asked. "Is she going to be in the pot too?"

"Probably not, she is handicapped and too big. They will do it when she is sitting."

And so it proved when they had finished with the boy and had wrapped him back up, it was the girl's turn.

Her robe was loosened and pulled down to reveal her shoulders and arms. The priest poured the water over her head three times and then anointed her with oil. Just like the boy, she was covered in crosses all over her body. It was a charming ceremony watched by proud parents and relatives. It was something a bigger child would never forget their entire lives.

Sean remembered even the smell of the oil that had covered him in the hotel bedroom. This wasn't done to stop the devil from getting in; this had been done to let love in.

This was also something memorable that would live with him forever.

This old religion obviously meant something serious and real to these people. The fear of the devil was obviously concrete to them. Icons of the Saints and Holy family gazing down on the scene confirmed that they were happy with what was happening. The Madonna smiled as she held her infant son.

St Paul's words to the Corinthians were understood in the context.

When I was a child, I spoke as a child, I understood as a child, I thought as a child: but when I became a man, I put away childish things.

For now, we see through a glass, darkly; but then face to face: now I know in part; but then shall I know even as also I am known.

Surrounded by so much religion, the two lads at the back became thoughtful and serious. There was something more going on here than met the eye. They needed to think about it.

Making a discrete exit, they left and found themselves back in the blinding sunlight.

They sauntered across the square to a restaurant holding hands. It felt good to be back in the sun and warmth.

"I wasn't expecting that," said Steve, looking closely at his quiet friend.

"No, it was a surprise, but a good surprise. It's good to see so many family members at a ceremony like that. I've been to a few christenings in Britain but they weren't as intense as that. I think we could do with a drink after all that."

They soon arrived in the restaurant and enjoyed a glass of wine while waiting for their meal. They watched as the congregation left the church and gathered in the square. It felt good to have played a small part, albeit unintentionally, in the Greek life and to feel that they understood it a bit better.

Some of the family members came into the restaurant and called for ouzo. It promised to be a long afternoon. After the meal and a few more glasses, Sean was beginning to feel tipsy.

"You know this place is starting to feel like heaven to me. Beautiful island, good weather, good-looking men everywhere. What more could a girl ask for?"

"You're drunk but yes, I agree with you. Are you glad we came here?"

"Of course, I am not sure if I want to go back," said Sean,

"That's always a sign of a good holiday but back we must go to the pub and brewery. Graham, Angie, Brian, and the old Stag's Head."

"It feels like a million miles away from all this," said Sean, indicating the christening party.

"Yes, and we're half-way through our first summer together. It's been a hell of a year so far," said Steve.

"We'll come back here one day and relive when we're old and grey," said Sean. "We'll walk through the harbour on our Zimmers or I'll push you in your wheelchair, and remember the time when we made love on the beach."

"And go to bed at nine o'clock with our cocoa mugs and help each other with our shoes and socks," laughed Steve.

"Yes, imagine that. I can't imagine you as an old man. Somehow you will always be thirty-something to me."

"Not so much of the something. You will grow old like ordinary men grow old, but hopefully, we will have each other to take care of. I want to grow old with you by my side," he said seriously, looking at Sean full-on waiting for his answer.

"Well, when you're sixty, I shall still only be fifty, so maybe then I'll look round for a younger model. Aren't you afraid I'll find my own toy boy to play with and leave you with your Zimmer."

"Not if I keep hold of you. I'll keep you satisfied. Why would you want a younger model? You will have trained me by then to cater for your every need and I'll be please to comply."

"Yes, you're enough for me, I reckon," said Sean. "You're not a bad catch after all, I could have done a lot worse."

"I'll take that as a compliment," Steve said, kissing his boy on the side of the head.

"We need an early night tonight. We've got a full day of travel tomorrow so we need to get some sleep," said Sean, finishing his drink.

Chapter 13

The journey back to the UK was uneventful.

They landed at Gatwick in the rain and got the train to Victoria after that Paddington. They gazed out at the sprawling fields in the drizzle. Their spirits were low, but once they reached Hereford, their spirits picked up and they were anxious to see their friends and the inn again.

"I hope everything is okay with the pub," said Steve getting into the taxi at Hereford station.

"Oh, I'm sure it will be. Graham and Brian know what they're doing. We've only been gone a week after all," said Sean.

As they pulled up outside the pub, a noisy altercation could be heard from within. They quickly paid the driver then took their bags inside. Graham was arguing with a young man at the bar who was saying that the beer had been watered down and was demanding another pint. Graham's face lit up when he saw Steve come through the door.

"Thank God, you two are back. I've had nothing but hassle all week since you left. This clown thinks we water down the beer; he's threatening to report us. Deal with it, Steve, it's doing my head in."

"What makes you think the ale is watered down, mate?" Steve wanted to know.

"It's weak as piss, that's why," said the farm labourer. Sean recognised him from school; the lad had been a bully there.

He was banned from half of the pubs in the neighbourhood and had tried this trick in most of them. Steve looked him straight in the eye.

"You're not getting another pint, mate, but nice try. I'll give you five minutes to down that and then fuck off, and don't come back."

The labourer was outnumbered and didn't like the sound of Steve's tone so he backed down, drank the rest of his pint and scarpered while his nose was intact.

"I dunno, we go away for five minutes and the place falls apart. Don't take any shit from these guys, they're just trying it on. Stand up to them and show them who's the boss," said Steve.

"Now I know why I went into business with you. How was your holiday?"

"Brilliant," said Sean, grabbing Steve in a hug from behind and lifting him off his feet. It felt good to be back.

Over the next few days though, both men started to get post-holiday blues. They missed the sun, blue skies, and the beaches. Watching the rain stream down the window on a Tuesday afternoon, they began to long for Cyprus.

"It's raining again. If we were in Cyprus now, we'd be having a drink on the terrace, watching the kids dive in the pool," said Sean mournfully.

"Yes," said Steve. "This country is great so long as you have the weather. Hey, I thought if we can't be in Cyprus, why not bring Cyprus here?"

"What do you mean?" Sean asked.

"We can have a Greek night retsina, ouzo, moussaka, bazooki; maybe a Greek stripper?"

"I'm not sure about the Greek stripper, unless we can persuade Lukas to get his kit off. There'd be quite a few who would pay to see that, me included," said Sean warming to the idea.

"I wonder if he could get his brother to come over, they could do a double act. I'll run it past Graham."

Graham loved the idea. He wanted to hold it in September during the harvest time, about the time of the harvest moon when the ghost of the hanged lad was due to appear.

"We could make it a fancy dress with a lot of Greek togas; a kind of early Halloween. Brian's mates would love any excuse to dress up." Sean's ears perked up at the mention of dressing up. The idea flew.

Like all good ideas, it came out of nowhere and it gathered a momentum of its own. The lads got in touch with Lukas who said he would be over and loved the idea of staying in a country pub. The chance of seeing the two English lads was a very exciting feeling. He wanted to bring his brother.

It was starting to be quite a night.

"Thanks for coming both of you. Welcome to the Stag's Head," said Steve, pouring them a drink.

"We've put both of you in the spare bedroom. Here, let me take your bags upstairs."

Steve recognised the red hold-all of Lukas, which contained the usual paraphernalia. It felt heavy.

The two Greeks unpacked and had a guided tour of the pub. They were impressed at how extensive it was. They asked about the stables and whether there were any horses available to ride.

"No, but we can arrange for you to go pony trekking if you want. Local farmers have half a dozen ponies that they hire out. There is quite a nice road to the wood on a nearby hill," said Steve.

"Do you and Sean want to join us?" Lukas asked with a twinkle in his eye.

"I'll ask him."

Sean was up for the idea and went to search for suitable riding gear. He had to look the part. After lunch, they went to the nearby riding centre by car where four ponies had been prepared for them. Lukas was particularly skilled at riding as he was a rider in the army as part of their criminal duties. He took the larger mare.

Dino was on a white stallion and the other boys had greys. It was a cloudy overcast afternoon but they were all in good spirits as they set along a well-marked route for the nearby hill of a lower bluff. It had a small wood on top. They sat off with a clatter of hooves on the farmyard cobbles.

The horses were calm and gentle. Lukas seemed a bit bored by the pace so he suggested to try to gallop. The horses were reluctant at first as they were only used to a walking pace but the four lads soon got a sweat up.

The four horsemen dug their heels into the horses' flanks and aimed for the hill.

Many horsemen had cantered over those green fields. During the Civil War, gay Cavaliers and dour parliamentarians had spurred their mounts on in a similar fashion. The woods and fields then though rang out to the cries of panic and alarm. No such noise was heard from our gay cavaliers.

They shouted in joy at the scenery around them.

Over a couple of fields, they rode. The sheep looked up in curiosity at the unexpected noise, and then ignored them and got back to the nibbling the grass.

The view over Herefordshire towards the golden valley was impressive. A patch work of green, brown and yellow justified the fertility of the land. Every piece of ground was being farmed. Only towards the top of the hills where tractors couldn't go was the land left to grow wild. The horses' dug in the soft ground and left marks for the birds to examine later.

The harvest was about to take place and not even the greyness of the weather could hide the luxuriousness of the crops as they swelled in preparation. Orchards of cider apples stretched far into the distance. At one point, the boys rode through an orchard and admired the crop of apples turning red slowly. Tractors were in the fields moving large bundles of straw to storage.

The countryside hummed with activity. This was the busiest time of year when all the hard work was going to be repaired. Nature was co-operating and playing its part this year.

The four horsemen pulled up just before the wood.

"Shall we go inside?" Dino asked, practising his English.

"Yes of course. We can dismount and let the horses have a breather," said Steve.

All four dismounted and started to walk up into the wood.

The wood was quiet except for the sound of one or two pigeons. The trees were full and the leaves were rustling slightly in the breeze. The two Greek lads led the way in, both of them looking magnificent in jeans and check shirts. They both wore leather belts and trousers.

"Are you looking forward to the party tomorrow night?" Sean asked.

"Yes," said Lukas. "Very much so. Do you want us to do anything for you tomorrow?"

"That would be good of you," said Steve. "There will be a lot of people there. Could you help Angie out with the food? I know you work in a cafe but it would help us enormously. Perhaps you could find some sexy waiter clothes for you to wear. Would you mind dressing up a bit?"

"No problem, it will be fun."

As they walked further into the wood, it got darker and cooler. They could make out a small, circular Greek-style temple in a clearing. The path led straight to it. It was obviously a folly built, perhaps in the 18th century by someone who had been on his European grand tour and had come back with the idea of building a small temple in the wood. It didn't look out of place but it was unexpected.

All four men were drawn to it. It was a perfectly circular building of stone with a large opening on one side. Post the opening overlooked the fine expanse of Herefordshire countryside just travelled over by the four lads.

Dino tied their horses to branches and let them graze. They approached warily. The cooing of the wood pigeons had stopped and there was silence around the temple. They had no idea what could be inside, if there was anything inside. It looked as if it was built to contain something.

Lukas was the first to go in. It was a bit gloomy inside but they could make a remarkable statue of what looked like a

199

naked teenage boy. It was made of marble and could have represented I am Dionysus. There was a jar at his feet. The boy was staring at the opening. With his blind eyes, he stared at the expanse of scenery through the trees.

The men approached and just regarded the youth. They admired his beauty and strength. The sculptor had sculpted him in a standing position fists, slightly closed but looking relaxed. His ridiculously small penis and scrotum were almost hidden in foliage of pubic hair.

They moved around to the back of the statue to admire the strong curved back and buttocks of the lad. He seemed to be challenging them, tempting them, mocking them; even a piece of stone frozen in an erotic stance.

"It's been well done," said Sean.

"Yes, he is beautiful," said Steve. The veins in the boy's arms could still contain blood and it give him a reality that impressed them.

Dino and Lukas conversed in Greek for a while but in a low tone, as if they were in church. All the men found it hard to leave the boy and to pull away, but then finally they did it, looking back at him before going out.

"I didn't expect to find that," said Steve.

"No, it's a real find. We'll come up here again now that we know he's here. He seems a bit lonely in there," said Sean.

"No electric fires to keep him warm," said Steve, remembering the young lad in the church.

They remounted and galloped back through the damp wood and the fields. When they got near the riding centre, they still looked back at the little wood on the hill.

Back at the pub, chores had to be carried out like cleaning the outside toilets.

"I'll do it," said Sean, eager to be seen to be doing something useful. He got a bucket of hot soapy water and took it outside to clean the toilet. It was the part of the pub that tended to be overlooked as people always thought someone else had done it. He went to the cubicle expecting to first wipe the toilet over.

A drawing on the back of the door caught his eye. Someone had drawn the picture of a lad being fucked by a large cock. Sean's name was scratched in the wood next to it as the lad being fucked. Word was out in the neighbourhood about him and Steve. He wasn't surprised it was difficult to keep that sort of thing quiet. He called out to Steve to come and have a look.

"What's the matter?" Steve said, coming up from the cellar.

"Come and look at this. Some twat has drawn a picture with my name on it."

Steve looked at it and dismissed it as not worth worrying about. "He's given me a big cock if that's supposed to be me," he laughed.

"But is that what people think of me?" Sean said. "Some sort of shag bag. It's disgusting."

"Hey, don't let it upset you," said Steve. "It's probably some stupid kid dying to get shagged himself. He's jealous that's all."

"Mm, I'm not so sure. Do you think we should tell people we're a couple now, get it out in the open? It might stop these sort of thing then."

"If you want to, I'll support you in anything you want to do. I'll put an ad in the Times if you want."

201

"Be serious. Yeah, it's time, isn't it? Let's do it tonight at the party. It would make a great story."

"I'm not getting on my knees with a ring though," said Steve.

"Spoilsport. You almost want to make an honest woman of me," he said.

"Certainly not," said Steve. "I prefer you as my slut. Now finish the job, get your knickers down and get upstairs for a shag."

"Cunt," was the only reply.

Sean tried to make out that he wasn't upset by the drawing but it played on his mind all afternoon. *Wonder who could have put it there. Could it have been Brian playing a joke?* He dismissed that idea; he wasn't that childish.

Could it have been Angie? No, not her style. He was perplexed by it. He hated the idea of people talking about them behind their backs but he argued that people will always do so, especially in a village setting. It would be better to bring their relationship into the open, after all this was the 1990s, not the dark age before it was legal.

What they were doing had been legal back in the sixties and plenty of young men and women were doing it these days. There was an age gap between him and Steve of just over ten years but the relationship was natural and easy. They were relaxed in each other's company and they did love each other. They had let Lukas into their life that one time but that was out of an overwhelming sense of curiosity rather than lust.

He justified it in his own mind as a turn-off along the main road to visit a peculiar church that was reputed to have another wonderful gargoyle on it! They were definitely worth a look. He put it out of his mind, for now, he had things to do.

By five o'clock preparations were nearly complete. The DJ was set up and the jockey was due to arrive at seven o'clock. The food was all prepared and laid out in the kitchen as there wasn't enough room in the bar. By seven, the first guests were arriving.

As it was fancy dress, a succession of ghouls and ghosts got tipsily out of taxis and noisily made their way inside. A few Greek togas got ripped in the short journey from taxi to the bar. The lads from the rugby club arrived in the mini-bus and had obviously been drinking already. Most of them were UN imaginatively dressed as farm yokels.

A couple of their girlfriends looked like milking maids. Graham had played centre for a couple of seasons and knew most of them. The bar filled up and the lads were kept busy for an hour also dealing with drinks. An ex-girlfriend of Graham turned up quite tipsy.

"Carol, what are you doing here?" Graham asked.

"Getting pissed, I hope. I've been looking forward to this all day. How are you? Haven't seen you around much, you old fart."

"No, been busy here, love. Found yourself a new fella yet?"

"I wish but looking at this lot, you never know. Maybe it's my lucky night tonight. Some of these rugby fellows are gorgeous. It's great that you have organised this. Was it your idea?"

"Not really. It was Steve and Sean's idea. They have been to Cyprus for a holiday. They felt a bit low when they came back so they organised a Greek night."

"What a disappointment that Steve was. I went out with him one night, he's like a bloody ice cube. There was more

203

passion in a beer mat. I couldn't get anywhere with him. We ended up going home early. Where is he by the way?"

"He's in the cellar putting a new barrel on. You know he is gay, don't you? Sean is his boyfriend. They've been an item for a few months now."

"I guess he batted for the pink team. It was his after shave, it was two sweet."

"You don't miss much, do you? So now you know. I love your costume by the way. What is it? Marie Antoinette?"

"Something like that. It started out a little Bo Peep but I got carried away."

"What do you want to drink, love? The first one's free."

"Then I will have a double brandy."

"You haven't changed much, have you?" Graham said, pouring a large one into a glass.

"Have a good night darling speak to you later."

Carol tottered off into the crowd and found a seat next to a rugby player. The atmosphere was building up. It was quite noisy in the bar. The fairy lights were twinkling on and off even though it was still light outside. The DJ hadn't shown up so Brian was drafted in to do the DJing; there was a lot of riding on him tonight.

It was better for Brian to do the DJ because if Steve had done it, he would have played Frank Sinatra all night. Brian had done it before on countless occasions in the student union bar. Even on one occasion when the local hells-angels chapter turned up, stripped off and cartwheeled around naked all night.

The sight of all those distended bear bellies and shrunken willies still haunted him at night. It took some time for the bouncer to get rid of them. He got on the mike.

"Kalu Sera, Kalu Sera. Good evening and welcome to our Greek night at the Stag's Head. We're going to have a great night tonight with your help. Are you ready to party? (Huge roar) Then let's get started with Nana Mouskouri singing a traditional Greek ballad. Only joking, it's Frankie Goes to Hollywood's *Relax*."

It was a good choice to start. That heavy insistent beat got everyone going and the lyrics struck the right note.

The crowd joined in with the song and begin to coalesce as a group; heads nodded and togas swayed as the temperature rose. Brian was really professional that night and although there wasn't much room to dance, he chose songs that could be sung in the union. Then he played *Glad to be gay*, an iconic cheer went up, and Ryan shouted out, "Seanie, playing your song." Steve shot him an ugly look.

He just hoped Ryan wasn't going to spoil the party that night.

About eight o'clock, they ran out of bottled cider. Sean was sent to the cellar to bring a crate up. All the lights were on which was lucky because the bottles he wanted were right back at the bar and under a few crates of wine. He was getting to them when he felt someone behind him. It was Ryan, slightly drunk with his cock hanging out of his trousers.

"Hello, can I give you a hand?"

"What the fuck are you doing?" Sean said in a panic. "Zip yourself up, man. Steve's in the bar. What if he comes down?"

"Oh, come on, Sean. There's no one about. Come and give me a kiss, I know you want to."

"No, actually, I don't want to, you crazy bastard."

"Did you like the drawing I did of you in the toilet?"

"Oh, that was you, was it? I should have guessed. Only you could have been that childish. Are you jealous of me and Steve?"

"You and Steve, are you an item now?"

"Have been for a while. He's twice the man you'll ever be. He's bigger than you too."

He shouldn't have taunted Ryan. Ryan was drunk and dangerous and wanted sex badly. He moved towards the boy who was trapped by the crates. He forced himself on the boy and tried to kiss him. It was like Ken all over again and the boy leant away from him. He got the smell of whisky on Ryan's breath and he could see the erection diminishing fast.

"That's enough, Ryan, you prat. Let go of him."

Steve was behind him looking savage. He caught Ryan by the collar and turned him around. One punch to the chin was all it took to put Ryan on the floor. Steve stood over him eager to continue.

"This is the last warning you get, boy. Leave him alone and fuck off. Find another lad to suck your cock for you."

"All right, alright, just pushing my luck. No hard feelings?" He extended a hand up.

"No hard feelings, mate," said Steve as he squeezed the blood out of Ryan's hand. Ryan winced.

"I've had a soft spot for that boy of yours for some time," he said. "I'm sorry."

"No problem. I think we understand each other now."

He helped Ryan stand and post him out of the cellar.

"You alright?" He asked Sean.

"I am okay, just a bit shaken up. I tried to fight him off, Steve, honestly, I did."

"I know. I saw and heard what you said. You're a good lad. Come here."

They hugged and Steve kissed him.

"Tell me if he ever bothers you again. I might have to get really nasty with him. Meanwhile, where are those bottles? Can you manage a couple of crates?"

"I'll try, he's strong that bastard, very strong."

Sean was nervous all night. He had one eye on his job and another looking behind him in case Ryan pounced, but Ryan had got the message from Steve and had left early.

By now, the food was ready to be served and people trouped into the kitchen to receive it. Some took plates outside and ate it on the seats in front of the pub.

Salad with rice and chicken or pork. Kebabs of lamb with peppers and onion. Moussaka with salad. It was going a swing.

Angie moved to the back for a cigarette and but Brian had beaten her to it.

"It's going alright, isn't it?" She said lighting up.

"So far, so good. I hope the drag artist shows up though that one act I don't want to stand in for," said Brian, drawing on his cigarette.

"You're playing a blinder on the disco," she said. "Good job that you stepped in to cover."

"Yeah, I reckon I'm owed a break after all this," he said.

"Oh, I'm sure the boys will see you. Ok. College doesn't start for a week or so, does it?"

"Yes, it's my final year too. I've got to decide if I want to become a teacher or stay in the pub trade."

"Why would you want to teach?"

"It's another string to my bow. You never know if another reunion comes along, I might be grateful for teaching."

"Would you teach primary or secondary?" Angie asked.

"Primary, I think. The kids are more genuine at that age. If they're bored with your lesson, they'll show it."

"True, I'm still not sure whether to come into the pub trade full-time. Sean is here. It makes more sense for him to run the kitchen and me to help when they're under pressure like tonight."

"Sounds good, you've a good job as it is. Why give that up to come and work here?"

"Well, Graham wants the pub to be a family pub. Eventually, we will get married and have kids. This would be a great place to bring up a family. It would be a real family pub. But I think Steve wants it to be more of a gay up. The only problem with that is the location. Most pubs are in the city centre, not stuck in the middle of nowhere."

"The locals may not be happy to have them as a gay centre. Most people here are very conservative."

"Well, I think a few eyebrows have been raised tonight. Let's see how the Desirée goes down. She's here."

Round the corner came a stunning six foot two inch blonde. Her stage name was Desirée but her real name was Paul Reynolds. He was a male nurse by day and Drag Queen by night. He looked good as a woman but the voice gave it away. As soon as he opened his mouth, he turned heads in disbelief.

"Hello, darling, who's got a light? I am on next apparently as soon as the plates have been put away. Make sure they all get collected, otherwise they might throw them at me."

"You are not as bad as that, are you," said Brian.

"No, but half this lot have seen my act before, I am sure."

She took a cigarette from Angie and inhaled deeply. She had the cigarette in her long manicured fingers and Brian was impressed by the beautifully painted nails; they were a deep red colour. Her dress was sequined and caught the light of the harvest moon.

"Full moon tonight," she said. "I thought half of them seemed crazy. The rugby crowd have stripped down to their trousers already, won't take much to get that lot starkers. I went to school with some of them too. I hope you like my jokes, they might have heard them before."

"I don't think that will matter, love. The cruder the better if you ask me," said Brian, trying to stay positive.

"Thanks, love, you are a doll."

"And so are you," said Brian, throwing his stub away. He went back inside to help clear the dishes.

"You make a very attractive woman," said Angie, admiring the high heel shoes and the sexy stockings Desirée had on.

"Why thank you. It's nice to get some appreciation. It takes at least an hour to get ready. The hair is a wig, of course, and the makeup takes a while. Thankfully, I don't have to shave much my hair, doesn't seem to grow that much."

"Where did you get those full-length gloves from? You don't see too many of those about these days."

"Charity shop, love. Surprising what you can pick up there. I found some lovely hats for my Marlene Dietrich tribute; cheap too. Nobody really wants them these days; it's a pity."

Desirée finished her cigarette and threw it into the car park.

"Well, here goes, wish me luck."

"Yes, good luck, love. Take no prisoners."

Desirée went to get ready. She was being carried in by Dino and Lukas. They went out of the front door and waited for Brian to announce them.

"Right, you lot, we've got a double treat for you tonight. Not only do we have the Delectable Desire but we have her Greek bodyguards. Two real Greeks from Cyprus, Dino and Lukas."

On the signal, the doors flew open and there was Desirée on the shoulders of Dino and Lukas, perched on like a drunken parrot. She waved to the crowd as they cheered her entrance. The crowd loved the glitter force of. Dino and Lukas were naked except for the jock straps and they looked stunning. They put her down carefully and she took the mike.

As she sang her first song, *I am just a girl who can't say no* the two Greek lads stood by her like a kind of backing but without the singing. They had oil on their arms and legs, and looked like wrestlers from Turkey. Every now and then, Desire would flick her fan at the boys gently, sending whoops of delight in the audience. All eyes were on Desire.

She flirted with the boys and with the crowd. Most of her jokes were all about being gay. She picked on members of the audience, especially those going to the toilet, telling them not to be too long or she'd come after them.

"How big's your cock?" One drunken reveller shouted.

"How big? Will be big enough for your mouth, love."

There were hoots of laughter. The revellers shut up as she had an answer for all the banter. She had heard most of it before.

But when Brian moved to the keyboard while on stage, the audience knew something was about to happen. They hadn't rehearsed the song but he knew it because he had played it so often in the student union bar.

It was Desirée's version of Gloria Gaynor's *I will survive*. A song sung in every gay bar in the land. As soon as she started, the audience went quiet.

First, I was afraid, I was petrified.
Kept thinking I could never live without you by my side.
But then I spent so many nights
Thinking how you did me wrong
And I grew strong
And I learned how to get along.
And so you're back
From outer space
I just walked in to find you here
With that sad look up on your face
I should have changed that stupid lock
I should have made you leave that key
If I'd known for just one second…

The whole crowd knew what she was singing about; finding the wrong one, feeling used, abused and confused. Plato knew the difficulties.

"And so, when a person meets the half that is his very own, whatsoever his orientation, whether it's to young men or not, then something wonderful happens…"

He whom love touches not walks in darkness.

The party was still going strong at midnight and people showed no inclination to go home. Brian changed the tempo of the evening by playing slower numbers. Most of the nearby club heads scored, including the captain of the team who had his arm around a shy lad he had met. It was one of those nights. Desirée had gone home after her act as she had a shift to cover the next day.

At two o'clock, people were starting to catch taxis and lifts and were wishing one another a good night. Financially, it had been a success and Desirée was happy with the extra fifty pounds that Steve gave her. The bazooka player never showed up but he wasn't missed.

As the last guest left, the guys surveyed the wreckage of the party. Streamers, corks, bottles, and cigarette butts littered the floor. Glasses were everywhere and Dionysus had been mutilated at some time during the night, missing a vital part of his anatomy.

Someone had drawn a bra on Aphrodite.

"Well done, lads," said Graham. "Are you all right?"

"Yeah, a bit pissed though," said Steve, starting to collect empty glasses.

"Oh, leave all that, mate, we can do that in the morning."

"As much as I hate doing that, I think you are right. Leave it, Sean, let's go to bed."

"No trouble either," said Graham, "as far as I know."

"There was with Ryan but it got sorted."

"What happened to him?"

"He left early. Angie lock up and let's call it a day."

And at about three o'clock in the morning, as the inn slept in the bright harvest moon which made a brief appearance through the upstairs window facing the yard, an image of a young boy carrying a lamb could be made out moving along the corridor. It stopped briefly outside Steve and Sean's room where they lay in each other's arms fast asleep.

A sardonic smile played on the handsome boy's face. If he had been a Greek boy, he would have been wearing his marriage clothes, not the coarse woollen clothes of the period. There was something sad about this lonely shape as he glided silently by. He went as far as the end of the corridor, and as another cloud covered the brilliant moon, his image faded away and vanished for another year, while outside the silence of the rain-soaked fields was almost palpable.

The End